"This is the book you fall asleep ⟨...⟩ excited to get back to. A Cult Ma⟨...⟩ ⟨...⟩ so many memorable characters and phrases you'll want to grab strangers and read paragraphs to them."

— **KATHLEEN HANNA**

"I have always admired Brontez Purnell's writing, and this novel is his greatest achievement yet. Purnell is never careful, never evasive. He hits you with honesty, passion, painful humor and never stops."

— **MIKE ALBO**

"Brontez Purnell is foul-mouthed and evil. Be warned: this book will make you cackle out loud like you've got the Devil inside you then it will break your heart. Be careful where you read it. BUT DO READ IT."

— **JUSTIN VIVIAN BOND**

"With epic detail and crude truth, Brontez Purnell reminds us that the lessons of survival and love are learned through life's most fucked-up circumstances. Brontez has written a story that helps us laugh, grieve, and breathe.

— **CRISTY C. ROAD**

"*Since I Laid My Burden Down* has a fearless (sometimes reckless) humor as Brontez Purnell interrogates what it means to be black, male, queer; a son, an uncle, a lover; Southern, punk, and human. An emotional tightrope walk of a book and an important American story rarely, if ever, told."

— **MICHELLE TEA**

amethyst editions

since i laid my burden down

brontez purnell

FEMINIST
PRESS
AT THE CITY UNIVERSITY
OF NEW YORK
NEW YORK CITY

Published in 2017 by the Feminist Press
at the City University of New York
The Graduate Center
365 Fifth Avenue, Suite 5406
New York, NY 10016

feministpress.org

First Feminist Press edition 2017

This book was made possible thanks to a grant from New York
State Council on the Arts with the support of Governor Andrew
Cuomo and the New York State Legislature.

Second printing September 2020

Cover and text design by Drew Stevens
Cover photo: *Untitled #301*, from the series The Parts by Evie Leder,
© 2016; courtesy of the artist.

LIBRARY OF CONGRESS CATALOGING-IN-PUBLICATION DATA

Names: Purnell, Brontez, author.
Title: Since I laid my burden down / by Brontez Purnell.
Description: New York : Feminist Press, [2017]
Identifiers: LCCN 2016047025 (print) | LCCN 2016054862 (ebook) | ISBN
  9781558614314 (softcover) | ISBN 9781558614321 (Ebook All)
Subjects: LCSH: African American men—Fiction. | Self-realization—Fiction. |
  Gay men—Fiction. | Domestic fiction. | BISAC: FICTION / African American
  / General. | FICTION / Gay. | FICTION / Family Life.
Classification: LCC PS3616.U785 S56 2017 (print) | LCC PS3616.U785 (ebook) |
  DDC 813/.6—dc23
LC record available at https://lccn.loc.gov/2016047025

Hate is a strong word, but sometimes it's not a strong enough word. DeShawn hated this.

He knew what had brought him back to Alabama. It was all that drinking, drugging, and fucking all those fucking worthless men. It was not any one catastrophe in particular, but all his failures in general. His uncle's death was just happenstance.

DeShawn got the call while in bed, in California: *Your uncle is dead.* The sentence punched him in the stomach, hard. He stayed in bed for two days, got up, packed, got on a plane, landed in Nashville, and drove an hour straight to the church. It was tucked deep in the woods, through the cotton fields, and sat on a grassy hill. The creek where he had been baptized almost thirty years earlier ran at the bottom of the hill. He remembered the cold, dirty water, and the preacher with one leg dunking him underwater like a little rag doll.

DeShawn peeked into the church he grew up in, and was shocked by how much hadn't changed. Maybe it was even moving backward. He entered and was handed a fan by the ushers, the same kind he was handed some thirty years ago as a little boy. It had a wooden handle with a picture of Martin Luther King Jr. or Frederick Douglass or Booker T. Washington. He couldn't believe they were still using these fans, which were a symbolic gesture, as they really didn't protect one from the oppressive humidity. Plus, the church had central cooling. As a child in the late eighties, a time before the church had an air conditioner or even a PA system, they only had the fans in the subtropical summer heat. That heat was a nuisance. As a child he would sit on the first pew and look back at the sea of black faces, all frantically fanning.

Before the coming of the PA system, the church choir's prerequisite was not that one could actually sing, but that one could project their voice to the back of the church. For this reason, DeShawn had led many songs in the children's choir. He couldn't carry a tune to save his life, but he could project. These things become metaphors for life if you're not careful. DeShawn learned it well; projection of voice was everything—be it literal or on paper—as was judicious use of its divine opposite, silence.

DeShawn sat some twenty feet from his uncle's body and thought about how all open-casket funerals are a son of a bitch. DeShawn told his mother, should anything happen, he wanted to be cremated. "Where do you want your ashes thrown?" asked his mother. "IN THE EYES OF MY ENEMIES!"

There had been this hysterical disease in his family's bloodline. Growing up, DeShawn watched his granddad and uncle behave like unchecked crazy people. The two men were often drunk, overly emotional, usually crying, exceptionally hysterical, and easily excitable. He remembered that his uncle and granddad had come to blows once when Uncle was eighteen because Granddad wouldn't let him have the puppy he wanted. All hell broke loose, people took sides, and it ended in a fistfight, a bloody nose, and a gun being pulled. Some children were more susceptible to the hysteria than others. DeShawn grew up and caught the family bug like a motherfucker. Sitting in the church with his baby nephew on his lap, DeShawn wondered if he was going to be a stark raving lunatic too. Only time would tell. He cried and held the baby closer.

Uncle was goddamn handsome as all hell,

and hypermasculine. Little DeShawn would wait for him on the porch to get home from high school. He drove a green '67 Dodge pickup truck. As a little boy, DeShawn would peek at him in the bathroom trying to see him naked. *That's what a man is.* Now Uncle really was dead. He was only forty. He'd had cancer since he was thirty-two, but refused to quit smoking. He couldn't be bothered, really.

The congregation began to rustle in preparation for Sister Pearl. Sister Pearl had been the choir headmistress for forever and a day. She claimed many times that she lost her voice singing for the devil. Sometime in her twenties she decided she wanted to sing the dirty blues, like Aretha Franklin. She quit the church and started singing along the Chitlin Circuit in Chattanooga, Nashville, Louisville, and on up to Chicago. One day, she said, the Lord took her voice away, and that's when she returned to church. Even as a boy, DeShawn modeled his singing voice after Sister Pearl's. It wasn't pretty—it was real. It sounded scratched, beaten, and pulsing with conviction, like she was trying to expel something. DeShawn didn't care much for her "devil" explanation; like any unrepentant prodigal son, he held that running away with the devil was highly underrated. Sister Pearl's voice lifted, and she sang "Since I Laid My Burden Down," the same song she'd sung at his baptism when he was five.

As the processional to the graveyard began, DeShawn's Auntie Margret got the spirit in her something fierce. She fell to the ground and started screaming, grabbed the casket and wouldn't let it go. Auntie set off the spark and everyone in the goddamn church lost it; it was a symphony of screams and hollers. Somehow, they made it to the graveyard. DeShawn saw the grave marked JATIUS McCLANSY and a chill ran though him. But Jatius was a memory for later. He looked away, down the hill to the creek. His baptism was the memory for right now.

DeShawn remembered being five and standing on the steps of the church in a matching white baptism gown and headwrap. All around him the adults were wearing white too. His grandmother kissed his head, and they made the procession down the hill to the creek. Some were holding lit white candles. Two of his girl cousins held his hands, the adults around him holding candles leading him on down to the creek and his uncle, who was chasing away any snakes or snapping turtles that might be lingering. The preacher at the time had lost his right leg to diabetes and had to be helped into the water. He recalled a floating feeling as he was brought midway into the creek to meet his uncles, who were deacons in the church, and the one-legged preacher. "This child has believed with his heart and confessed with his mouth," said the preacher as he covered DeShawn's face and pushed him under the creek water; it was cold as hell. DeShawn stood there, submerged, a feeling he could in no way explain.

Up on the bank, Sister Pearl let out a song.

Burden down, Lord.
Burden down.
People don't treat me like they used too since I
    laid my burden down.
Every round goes higher and higher . . .

DeShawn's little soul popped right back up out of the water, feeling cold and wet and not as new as he thought it would.

CHAPTER ONE

Before DeShawn left for Alabama and before his uncle's death, others had gone. For instance, Arnold was dead. Dead, dead, dead as Latin. He sunk with the Titanic. He flew the coop. That monkey had gone to heaven. It seemed that all the wild men around him were dying faster than he could keep track. Arnold was not the first, but he was of note.

DeShawn received the message on the morning train, on the way to classes in Oakland, and he hopped on the next train back to nowhere. There was nowhere to mourn the dead boy. Arnold had not lived in any one place for long, and had pulled so much shit that no one really loved him that much anymore. Or maybe they were waiting to love him again after he climbed out of the hole he had dug himself. Like he would appear out of thin air, a magician's assistant with a tiara and a sash that said "Healed" or something. The dead boy died before completing that magic trick. He would be that type of memory: one to forget. Three days of crying ensued and then a phone call. Arnold's final roommate called DeShawn and asked very sweetly if he would clean the dead boy's room. DeShawn said yes.

This would be his last favor to Arnold. He had loved Arnold. No one knew they were fucking, and from outward appearances it probably seemed like a casual camaraderie. Fucked-up boy loves even more fucked-up boy. It was rainy, and DeShawn showed up with supplies to clean the dead boy's room.

There were old clothes, new needles, crack pipes, Lorca poetry, and books by Bukowski. The dead boy was gentle-featured and very, very handsome. He had tried to get clean this last time, couldn't, and then stepped in front of a car.

DeShawn's mind shifted to his faraway youth, a certain redneck boss with permed and teased hair, smoking and sharing her thoughts on suicide. She said, "If you are brave enough to jump off a building or shoot yourself in the head then you are BRAVE. ENOUGH. TO. LIVE."

He took it as truth because an adult had said it. And he had believed it, up until the point that he knew someone who stepped in front of a car. Up until the point he stepped in front of that car, Arnold had not been a brave person. He was fatigued, and he had made a choice. DeShawn stood over an unopened jig-saw puzzle. He wondered what Arnold felt the moment that car struck him. Had he regret-ted it? DeShawn believed in energy, and he believed in the other side. He lit candles, paid respect to the eight corners, and prayed—that is, hoped—that the gentle, handsome departed boy was resting in power. He asked whatever god was listening to hear him on this. He set up Arnold's altar—a white candle and a glass of water—on the highest point in his room.

There were, of course, people around town who liked to talk. They called the handsome dead boy a junkie, and after that they called him a thief. This was true. "He was also a loved child of God," offered Arnold's mother. Maybe this was also true.

Away from the talkers and gossipers was Arnold and DeShawn's criminally minded and largely harmless inner circle. It is a beau-tiful thing to surround oneself with people who have pulled too much sketchy shit to ever judge anyone. The type of people you could fuck over, as long as you prove it wasn't any-thing personal. Everything around Arnold went missing—rent money, LPs, stamp collec-tions. Naturally, there was some resentment. But then again, everyone saw in Arnold a brother who was in deep pain. Which made his trespasses not forgettable, but forgivable. Somewhere, Arnold had his wings.

But there was still the matter of cleaning the room. DeShawn knew he couldn't clean it all at once. It would take days, and that was fine. There wasn't the dead boy's laughter to hear on the phone anymore. There wouldn't be his physical presence in the room, by the window strumming a guitar or smoking, or standing naked, with the most beautiful erection you could imagine. The place where Arnold's life made a rude exit was now a black hole, a deterioration in the film loop. This void meant there was time. Cleaning up a mess takes time. DeShawn knew that in order to clean up the dead boy's room, like, to *really* clean it, he would have to put on the armor of detachment. Detachment was a beautiful thing. You needed detachment to be nonjudgmental. He didn't want to say that Arnold was a selfish piece of shit for dying. He wanted to feel noble about it. He stayed neutral and nonjudgmental as a strategy to keep moving, a bargaining tool to keep the darker thoughts at bay. But people make judgments. It's the first thing people do.

DeShawn had loved about a hundred tragic motherfuckers, and this boy was no exception. Loving this type of man meant not having opinions, judgments, or expectations. It meant being practiced in just letting things "be." DeShawn internalized all of the boys, their fears, hopes, and mistakes. He studied them so hard he didn't see them anymore, he only saw himself. This was either a beautiful thing or the same mistake all deep empaths make. Judging any of the tragic boys he loved would mean judging himself. It already seemed exhausting. That said, he wanted to channel the dead boy's feelings, the adrenaline pumping through him. What *had* he felt like when he walked in front of that car? The second he moved forward, had he regretted it? Or did he feel some form of relief?

People tend to navigate from experience. DeShawn himself had never thought of suicide, but he could understand ennui, that feeling of life as perpetual and epic but mostly for no big reason. On those really hard days DeShawn felt like a single sperm swimming around in some gay dude's butthole, searching frantically for an egg that just wasn't there. But suicide? Never. Homicide? Yes. *Fuuuuuuuuuuuuuuuuck yes*, he thought. The thought of killing some rude, deserving asshole was so orgasmic it gave him a boner. But, of course, this was just a thought. Killing someone felt like a really complicated math equation. There were time variables, x's and y's, and where would you dispose of a body these days? A killer had to be self-sufficient and clean up his tracks. A suicide victim leaves a mess for someone else to clean up. He wondered if the EMT worker who cleaned Arnold's body from the highway had felt a certain way about it, or if he just saw a job as a job. It's surely never pleasant to see a body obliterated six ways to Sunday, but after the hundredth time, certainly something had to change. As a rule, as time passes all trauma has the potential to cool off in one's mind.

• • •

Under a pile of exhausted art supplies, DeShawn found Arnold's Nirvana shirt. It smelled like hell and sparked more memories than he cared for. Besides being one of Arnold's favorite bands and one of his favorite shirts, there was the historical baggage loading it down. DeShawn remembered April 4, 1994. He was in sixth grade. He remembered a cold and windy pre-spring day, and his hatred of the school bus that dropped him off at home. He remembered turning on MTV and fucking losing it. Kurt Loder was on the screen; Kurt Cobain had killed himself. Shot himself right in the head.

In seventh grade, DeShawn ditched Sunday school and Bible study and started running with his middle school's premiere group of headbanger girls, Margret Lopez, Amelia Andrews, R'ella Bollers, and one girl whose name he couldn't remember. A year to the date of Kurt's death the crew held a Satanic séance under the stairs by the drama room—a very, very failed effort to raise the spirit of Kurt Cobain. DeShawn didn't care about the séance being not so successful; he was just happy that these girls had invited him in and stamped his cool card. They wore all black, smoked weed, were sort of sexually active (Margret was rumored to have been fingered the summer before), and they practiced Satanism. How fucking cool was that?

It was a rather poor séance. The coven ducked under the stairwell in as much of a circle as the space would allow. Margret lit a black candle and laid a picture of Kurt on the ground. Everyone (except DeShawn) was wearing black lipstick. They all held hands and *believed together*.

It became apparent to DeShawn (after two minutes) that he had no fucking clue as to what "sign" they were waiting for to tell them that Cobain had indeed intercepted their message in the spiritual realm. All he knew was that after another minute of *believing*, the bell rang and they were tardy to class and certainly facing detention.

They had left the stairwell feeling defeated. Why hadn't Kurt answered them?

Now, in all small towns people talk. One of DeShawn's bitch-ass Christian cousins ratted to his mom that he was hanging out with white girls who worshipped Satan. His mother, furious per usual, showed up to his room that night with a belt, foaming at the mouth. "ARE YOU A HEADBANGER?! DO YOU BE AT SCHOOL BANGING YOUR HEAD?!" She had said *headbanger* with the salty peculiarity of a woman saying, with active disdain, a word she never knew existed. She beat his ass, took all his Nirvana records, and left to spend the night at her boyfriend's house.

The little hero inside DeShawn stood post–ass beating, all rage, his body covered in red welts. He was trying hard to catch his breath. "MY MOM IS SUUUUUUUUCH A BITCH!" In one statement, a whole new life began. In a plot twist that he would figure out when he was older, DeShawn experienced an epiphany. He didn't like Nirvana because he knew what the fuck Kurt was talking about. He liked Nirvana because it pissed off his bitch-ass mom. Hell, hell, rock and roll. The devil's music was still doing its job, still prompting kids to leave a nowhere life. The night of getting his ass beat by his mom would crescendo into a body of work, community, purpose.

Now those kinky banger girls from middle school were posting pictures of kids on the computer screen, a view into their normal lives. They lived in places like Texas and Kansas. They had houses now, and families. DeShawn looked up and all he knew were musicians. Every boy he had ever loved had been either a musician or a drug addict. Usually both. It was a yucky realization. But it kept to certain themes in his life, of stubbornness, of going longer, harder, of always being the last to leave the party.

"I want off this ride," he said, really, *really* meaning it this time.

• • •

He didn't want to be at this party by himself. He looked at the whirling vortex of the room. He felt like someone's mom, minus the tits and the patience. He didn't know whom to blame for the boy's death—maybe nineties MTV? DeShawn couldn't pinpoint exactly who it was that sold him and his buddies the idea that they were all gonna do a bunch of drugs and be rock stars one day. Selling this notion was like selling cigarettes to kids. *I guess they sell kids cigarettes too,* he reasoned.

Another angle was that Arnold and DeShawn had two different parental realities.

Arnold's parents were too high and checked out to check in with him, whereas DeShawn's main parent, his at-times single mom, could be humorless and perma-sober — the type where a child might wish a parent would develop a drug habit to calm them the fuck down — but she checked in. All history aside, he still didn't fully understand why Arnold was dead and he was still standing.

Within three days he finished cleaning the room and saying goodbye to Arnold. Arnold was DeShawn's second lover to die, maybe not the last. He was still young.

• • •

Men become pieces of shit either because they've had their ass beat too much or because they've never had their ass beat a day in their life. Prime example was DeShawn's first "boyfriend," Jatius McClansy. Jatius had his ass beat every day of his life and that's what killed him.

John McClansy was Jatius's younger brother and DeShawn's archnemesis. They played in the cotton field behind his boyhood house, and as far as John was concerned, it was always open season on DeShawn's ass. He would hurtle dirt clods at his head and call him "faggot" so much that DeShawn started to believe he indeed was one. Sometimes when John beat him up, both boys' mothers would come out to stop the commotion. DeShawn didn't understand it at the time, but behind all this animus was competition, plain and simple. John hated the way his older brother favored DeShawn. Whenever the neighborhood boys played ball, Jatius would stop to help DeShawn with his throw. He'd take him on walks in the woods, or help him when his bike had a flat. In a neighborhood where dads were scarce—DeShawn's own mom had been divorced from his stepdad about two years—male attention was a commodity, and DeShawn would sense this competition well into his adult gay life.

Jatius McClansy was what you would call a specimen. By the age of fifteen he looked like a right grown man—beard, muscles, chest hair, a towering six-foot-one frame, and a big and obvious bulge in his pants where a big and obvious bulge should be. Edna McClansy had quite a time keeping all the neighborhood single moms off her handsome son.

So it happened one summer, when DeShawn was eleven, that Jatius touched him in a way an older boy shouldn't touch a younger one. This excited DeShawn something crazy, but confused him too. Either way, he figured he didn't mind and that he wanted more. The McClansys lived behind DeShawn's backyard and up the cotton field. His mom would leave for her boyfriend's house, and DeShawn would leave his baby brother sleeping in his crib and go see Jatius. He would run up the cotton field and through the moonlight. He would run so fast beside objects so dark it felt like he was flying. White cotton against moonlight and fireflies. It looked a certain way.

That summer Jatius showed him his first porn. Jatius's dick was the first he touched. DeShawn grabbed it and was flush with it, the way he imagined a small stroke to feel. Later that summer DeShawn watched from a tree through Jatius's window as he had sex with T'resa Watkins. Jatius and DeShawn carried on up until the next summer, and then they would stop forever.

Edna was an overworked and overstressed single mother. One of the few women around with a college education, she had worked on the army base from the time she got pregnant with Jatius. You could imagine this woman's head hitting the glass ceiling so hard that blood was running down her face. She was a nervous woman. DeShawn remembered sleeping over at the McClansy's house once and Edna waking them up at 1:00 a.m. with a vicious racket. "YOU WORTHLESS BASTARDS. GET UP! GET THE FUCK UP! Y'ALL GONNA CLEAN THIS

DIRTY FUCKIN' HOUSE. YOU GONNA CLEAN THIS DIRTY FUCKING HOUSE UNTIL I GET TIRED!" DeShawn would understand later, as we always understand much later, why Jatius, despite being a teen sex god, also wore the look of a defeated man well before his expiration date.

And then, shit hit the fan.

Jatius worked as a cashier at the Piggly Wiggly. It was around the Fourth of July that Jatius was caught giving T'resa Watkins $126 worth of free meat through his checkout line. He got fired and everyone knew why. Edna came home from work early that day, and beat her son within an inch of his life. After she left the house, Jatius got her gun from her closet, went into his room, and blew away his brains.

DeShawn walked into Jatius's room a day and a half later. He walked past John, who was in the living room staring, silent and far away, at a wall. DeShawn's mother was among the neighborhood women consoling Ms. McClansy and cleaning the blood from the carpet. "It just wouldn't come up," his mother said in a tidy way as she was baking a pie for the funeral dinner.

She said one more very tidy thing.

"You don't kill yourself over a job at Piggly Wiggly," she spat, all glowing and prophetess-like, as she put the pie in the oven.

DeShawn, being the little ingenue he was, was still ignorant of the larger metaphors at work around him. He didn't know the world for what it was yet — one large, conniving god-damn Piggly Wiggly.

While silently watching his mother wrap tin foil around the other baked pies, he made a mental note of her implication.

It's okay to steal from grocery stores, but it's not okay to die.

CHAPTER TWO

Arnold's room was clean and he was buried, never to be forgotten. It was on to new heart-aches now.

DeShawn saw the streetlights turning on in the city and the fog rolling over the bay and coming through his bathroom window. He stood in the mirror and buttoned the last anchor-imprinted button on his pea coat. Then—uh-oh—one gaze at the mirror lasted a second longer than it should have, followed by another, then another. Now he was lost.

The same phenomenon would happen in his youth. He would glare into the mirror and ask, *Why do I look like this?* until the question was on repeat and he could not leave the stare in the mirror. It was self-hypnosis. Deep reflec-tions in the mirror, oftentimes while high, this time sober.

This particular hypnosis was filled with reflections about his self-imposed bachelorhood. There was a time, many years ago, when he held vague plans of marrying some well-behaved man, moving to the suburbs, adopting children, and calling it a day. This was before he really knew himself. There had been too many self-publicized stunts of him unabashedly *expressing* himself in public, not to mention all those photos of him getting fucked floating around the Internet. Any man remotely resembling husband material steered clear of him years ago. There was nothing left to do at this point but become a drag queen and own a lot of pets. DeShawn's impending drag queen–dom loomed over his head like college loan debt. He looked even deeper into the mirror, and the current of self-hypnotism spilled further inside him. *What will my drag name be? Ms. Fire? Essence Jostle? Cable Access? Precious Hyman?* The possibilities were endless, and for the first time that day the future was looking creative and bright, though there were more pressing matters at hand.

• • •

It had started innocently enough. He asked himself, *Who am I going to fuck tonight?* and went through his mental Rolodex until two well-hung Europeans came to mind: Sven and Michael.

Now, Sven was Swedish and charming in the same way an Ikea appliance was charming: a cute, lightweight, energy-efficient, and very replaceable piece of Euro bullshit. Sven personally annihilated all notions of Europeans being intrinsically more sophisticated because of a couple thousand more years of art and culture. He exclusively listened to rap music and he only ate at McDonald's. The first night they fucked, Sven asked, very charmingly, if DeShawn knew how to "make his ass clap like the black girls in the rap videos." Sven then offered DeShawn a hundred dollars to demonstrate. Before he knew what was happening, DeShawn was butt naked and frantically twerking over Sven's face, while Sven, also naked, was lying horizontally on the floor, face up, with a one-hundred-dollar bill erotically pressed between his lips. "More! More! Faster! Faster!" cried Sven. The whole time DeShawn thought, *Is this really fucking happening?*

But alas, Sven was back in Sweden for the summer. The other obvious choice was the German, Michael.

Michael was twenty-three years older than DeShawn and owned the anarchist bookstore in an alleyway near the train station. DeShawn was dubious as to how Michael kept the store open, particularly a bookstore selling anarchist ideas in a city where capitalism was winning more and more every day. He suspected rich parents, but never brought it up. The rule about fucking rich boys was you never, ever, under any circumstances, brought up their privilege. They hate that shit. Shut the fuck up and let them pay for dinner. He learned this lesson the hard way. And besides, Michael was generous.

"Michael, will you buy me a new record player?" asked DeShawn.

"Yes," said Michael.

"Michael, can I have a new coat?"

"Yes."

"Michael, can I have three hundred dollars for an art project?"

"Sure."

DeShawn had met Michael at an antiwar art show/protest some twelve years earlier. Michael learned that DeShawn was studying dance and asked him to come to his studio. He wanted to paint him naked.

"I don't know much about visual art," said DeShawn, undressing in the cold studio.

"Dancers," Michael said, giving DeShawn's naked body the once-over, "are indeed visual artists. You need to flip your thinking."

With that little bit DeShawn fell in love with Michael, and vice versa. They made love all night.

Michael had been married three times: once to a woman in his teen years, and twice since he and DeShawn started their thing. Michael's third marriage was to some young man, twenty-five years old and a student at the Art Institute. It came as a crushing blow to De-Shawn's ego. *Why didn't he ask me to marry him?* Not that he necessarily *wanted* to be married to Michael, but it's always nice to be asked.

DeShawn had been meeting Michael in the back room of the bookstore for ten years. One day he thought if he wasn't careful, it could turn into another ten years of fucking some dude's husband, and what would he have to show for it? Did he even need to have any-thing to show for it? DeShawn didn't envy Michael's new husband, this young boy who made shitty art and didn't know his ass from a hole in the wall, this young man who had mar-ried an aging, promiscuous anarchist. *Heaven help that boy*, thought DeShawn. There had been so many men for him to cry over; there wasn't really a reason for Michael to be one of them. He had Michael's love, his attention, his generosity. And so DeShawn continued to help the aging anarchist cheat on all his husbands.

They always had sex in the back room of the bookstore. DeShawn had his own key. "I'm not allowed to fuck other men in the house," Michael explained. All over the walls were worn yellow press clippings from when DeShawn was a young dancer in the city. Michael saved every one. DeShawn would stare at pictures of himself from a decade ago and wince a little. He was certain that the boy in those pictures didn't exist anymore. There was also the picture of Michael and his first wife in Germany, back when Michael was a teenager. DeShawn could barely recognize him. His hair was still black then and he wore a serious expression. His wife looked even sterner. DeShawn could only imagine their life together.

One time, after he had fucked Michael's brains out, DeShawn asked, curiously not maliciously, why Michael hadn't picked him to marry. Michael went on what sounded like a scripted rant about DeShawn being an artist and needing freedom and experience; he said love would only hold him back. "You're my strong, independent boy."

"I'm not as strong as you think I am," argued DeShawn.

This particular night DeShawn walked straight to the back room, unbuttoned his peacoat, and made his way to the bed where Michael was lying, already naked, on his stomach.

The physical connection between the two

was eternal, even as the emotional connection seemed shifty. Michael was still quite a specimen of a man.

DeShawn pressed his mouth on the opening of Michael's anus and began with his tongue. He alternated this with quick bites to his butt cheeks. Michael answered by raising his hips. DeShawn licked upward to the base of Michael's spine and then up, up, up. Still on his stomach, Michael whipped his head around to look DeShawn dead in the eye, as if to say *kiss me, please*. DeShawn obliged. He rubbed saliva on his dick and pressed the head into Michael's opening. Michael's anatomy opened up and DeShawn pumped to frenzy and completion inside of him. As they lay there afterward and napped, DeShawn said to himself, *This will never change, ever*. He didn't linger on it. He knew it was the type of heartbreak that would inevitably disappear.

DeShawn left the bookstore while Michael was still sleeping. He caught the last train to the other side of the bay and walked under the streetlights some three blocks before his front door; there, something weird caught his eye. In the partition of the road, where trees were planted, was a gold figure holding on to a tree. Or rather, a figure dressed all in gold holding on to a tree for dear life. It appeared to be an older black woman in a platinum blond wig, gold lamé windbreaker with matching bottoms, and gold-plated hooker heels. *What the fuck?* thought DeShawn.

"HAAAAAAAAAAAAAAAALP!" she yelled.

DeShawn ran over as she fell from the tree, spilled into the road, and started crawling. He helped her up. In the heels, she was a good five inches taller than DeShawn's five-foot-nine stature.

"I'm sixty-three! I'm a TRAAAAAAAAAN-SEXUAL, and I want to get fucked like a WOOOOOOOMAN!" she yelled. All DeShawn could think was, *Get in line, bitch.* She smelled like booze. She continued, "I don't like gay boys, I like MEN. Are you a gay boy, or are you a MAN?" DeShawn paused. Until then, it had never occurred to him in all his life that he was both.

"Does it matter?"

"Help me home, baby," said the Gold Woman. DeShawn took her by the hand and walked her the full seven blocks in the opposite direction of his house to her apartment. She fell down seven more times.

At the apartment a sketchy looking man at the door grabbed the old woman by her stomach and gave DeShawn a curious look. "Are you okay, Dorothy?" he asked.

"I'm fine," she said. "My little boyfriend is helping me home."

Once inside the building, she confided in DeShawn as she took her keys out of her bra. "That man is a monster! He tried to ravage me before! Who would take advantage of an old woman?!"

The older lady opened her apartment door. She had left the radio on in an attempt to deter burglars. She was old school. DeShawn looked at the two-room flat and noticed a dirty-ass kitchen and a middle room with a bed and a black-and-white TV playing an old Western. He felt like he had stepped into *The Twilight Zone. Like, what station was playing a Western at this hour?* He helped the woman to the bed. She undid her track jacket to reveal a gold lamé bra and nice tits. DeShawn was impressed. *Where did she get a matching gold lamé bra? American Apparel?* She went in for the kill.

"You a handsome gay boy. You sho' is handsome!"

She liked him all of a sudden.

She leaned in to kiss him and DeShawn let her. *I mean, I'm already here*, he thought.

"Here," she said. Wobbly, she stood and pulled down her track pants. DeShawn was expecting gold lamé panties, but was disappointed when all he saw was white cotton. But concealed in those white granny panties was one of the biggest, hardest dicks DeShawn had ever seen in his life. He was impressed that the old bitch could still get a hard-on while wasted, and at the ripe age of sixty-three. A feat DeShawn couldn't manage at nearly half the old broad's age.

Shit just got real, thought DeShawn.

She kept on stuttering, "You's a handsome gay boy, you's a handsome gay boy." She began to play with her dick. *Oh hell no, I'm not passing this shit up, NO FUCKING WAY*, thought DeShawn, and began suckling on that big-ass dick like a baby piglet on a teat. The older woman seemed to be enjoying it—"You's a handsome gay boy, you's a handsome gay boy"—then mid–blow job she passed out, and fell completely backward onto the ground, dick still rock hard. DeShawn, being the handsome (and greedy) gay boy that he was, entertained the notion of touching the woman's penis one last time (when would he ever get to play with a dick that big again?), but taking advantage of a passed-out, big-dicked lady was a line he decided he couldn't cross.

Well, that happened, he thought as he locked the door behind him and went home to sleep.

CHAPTER THREE

Drinking at the bar near his house in Oakland, memories of DeShawn's dead uncle had been on repeat in his head. He remembered riding in his uncle's '67 Dodge pickup, his uncle driving, totally fucking wasted off bourbon, with DeShawn and his two other cousins in the cab, all four gentlemen packed in like sardines. DeShawn must have been all of eight or nine.

"Y'all wanna see Uncle cut some donuts?!"

"Yes!" screamed all three little boys simultaneously.

Uncle raced the vintage pickup to a field and did just so. On the third 360-degree turn, ol' Uncle noticeably lost control of the truck, and that heart-stop, wait-for-disaster feeling flew through little DeShawn's body. The miscalculation proved not to be fatal, but there it was — the origin of that anxious feeling DeShawn would come to know all his life. That punched-in-the-lungs feeling of anticipation, moments before something spun out of control.

The last thing DeShawn remembered that night was getting kicked out of the bar.

In the morning, poor DeShawn woke up on the kitchen floor in front of the refrigerator, door wide open and all the evidence splayed out around him: a half-empty jar of peanut butter, a jam jar, a rice-milk container, and half a stick of unwrapped, salted, organic (delicious, delicious) butter with teeth marks in it. He was naked and there was peanut butter every-*fucking*where. *WAS I ATTACKED LAST NIGHT?!* he thought after jerking into consciousness. He faced up to it three beats of silence later; he had blacked out and was binge eating. Again.

He left the mess on the floor, showered, and arrived at work a full forty-five minutes late.

"Dude, fuck this place," he said as he looked around the shitty barbershop. He prayed for the courage to quit and become a drug dealer. He figured that maybe if he got put in jail he could finally find a boyfriend. He was feeling optimistic that day — maybe he was still drunk — but didn't want those positive feelings to float too high in this place. He knew feeling good was a setup, so he sat down and waited for his bitch-ass coworkers to fuck with him.

One of the hairdressers, Lucy, was this

nasty, fake leprechaun from some redneck part of California. She was the worst mix of born-again Christian and closeted homosexual. Her "husband" would come in to help her close, and from the looks of it, he suffered the same affliction. Sexually frustrated assholes as they were, DeShawn felt sorry for them. There was no reality whatsoever in which he could picture Lucy's husband dicking her down good in any tangible way. When DeShawn looked at Lucy's husband, he saw an anxiety-ridden homosexual with a hungry booty hole, and it takes one to know one.

Her husband's panic attacks were infamous (he had upward of three a week), and each time Lucy would come into work disgruntled, highly critical, and pissed at everyone. DeShawn was only a receptionist, so in accordance to natural law Lucy got to fuck with him. For instance, she once explained to DeShawn why the young black teenagers in the area made her uncomfortable; she got robbed by a group of them once. DeShawn didn't believe this cackling bitch one bit. The ironic part was that, in this gentrified part of town, the black teenager robbing you most likely came from college-educated parents—though DeShawn knew that Lucy's stuck ass would never see the humor in that. It also left DeShawn wondering, *What kid that comes from college-educated*

*parents would rob a sloppy white bitch in sweats?
Like, wouldn't you rob someone who looks like they
have a future?*

Then there was Lucy's lil' gay sidekick, Juan
Gomez. Juan was from redneck California too,
and he and Lucy would openly bond over
their fear of "outsiders." Once at a Christmas
party DeShawn got *way* too drunk and told
Juan about when he was gangbanged by four
tourists from Mexico City the night before at
the bathhouse.

"EWW! YOU FUCK MEXICANS?!" cried Juan
Gomez.

As DeShawn understood it, some gay guys
are pissed or crazy because they were molested
as children (as he knew from personal experience); on the opposite side of a completely
different coin were fags like Juan, who were
bitches because they were completely ignored
as children. Juan had taken to yelling at
DeShawn in front of customers, with Lucy
backing him. And with Juan's convincing five-
foot-two frame and high-pitched yelp, every
time Juan attacked him all DeShawn could
picture was being dry humped by a barky little dog—and not a very cute one at that.

Working at this barbershop was total bullshit. The phone rang off the hook like a goddamn headache all fucking day long; people
calling for trims for their ugly-ass kids and

hairdressers are the fucking worst. "You know, for people who just cut hair all day, they sure are some uppity bitches," DeShawn found himself remarking to the general ether often.

A month prior, DeShawn called his father crying. It was another morning where he woke up on the kitchen floor covered in condiments, empty food packages haloing his body. He told his father he was going to quit the barbershop. He forgot the way his father could derail things.

"Son, think about them child prostitutes in Thailand, do you think they like their job? But they still get up and go! You're a pussy!" And then the old man hung up on him.

DeShawn wanted to call him back and explain that there's no such thing as a "child prostitute" — these days they were referred to as "abused children." But he quickly remembered to never, *ever* call his drunk-ass dad.

It was his mother who would save his resolve.

Some lackluster morning — that of the incident that would get him arrested and fired — DeShawn had been in the shop doing two hundred different things. Of those two hundred things, he got four wrong and Juan laid into him in front of the customers again.

DeShawn felt that punched-in-the-lungs anxious feeling. In the three seconds before he leaped over the counter and beat that faggot's ass, he saw his life in freeze-frame. It was as if he were standing between two mirrors, his image projected a million times on both sides of him.

Which one is the real me? he asked himself curiously.

• • •

DeShawn was a man that understood our actions have consequences, but, just as important, so do our inactions. He learned this from his mother one time in church nearly twenty-plus years earlier.

Young DeShawn had seen his mother in this state before, almost too many times to count: hysterical, unflinching, an hour past giving a fuck. Like Joan Crawford driving Christina home after being expelled from school, rollers in hair and a death grip on the steering wheel, subtly swerving.

She had been fighting with both her husband and her boyfriend that week and was feeling herself. She was over it. She meant business. She wasn't having it.

In the car, driving fast and swerving, DeShawn's mother foreshadowed the coming storm. "I don't give a fuck if he's the preacher! He can't tell us what to do!"

His mother took issue with most of the new preacher's rules. DeShawn was the last person baptized in the creek. The new preacher didn't want to baptize in the creek anymore because of the farm next door.

"The pigs shit in it," explained the preacher.

As rational as it seemed, it was still another policy change that annoyed the fuck out of his mother.

This bitch is about to show the fuck out, thought DeShawn, butterflies racing in his stomach. He knew very well what his mother bear was capable of, and knew that it was going to turn into a total fucking shutdown.

Now, the new preacher was already corrupt as a Baptist minister. He slept with women in the congregation and embezzled money. DeShawn's mother took issue with a man like this making rules for anybody. The war started when he announced a new policy that forbade the church elders from dipping snuff during the service and spitting the run-off into their Dr. Pepper cans. The preacher thought this was against form and fashion, and decided to ban the practice.

DeShawn's mother thought the old people in the church, who had lived through Southern poverty, Jim Crow, and god knows what else, should have the right to dip a little snuff in church, for fuck's sake. They were to vote on the rule at the church meeting, but the term "voting" wasn't exactly accurate. It was an unspoken rule that the preacher's word was law and no one voted against him. Ever.

"All in favor of the new rule say, 'Aye,'" said the preacher, and everyone but DeShawn's mother obliged him. "Opposed?" he asked.

DeShawn's mother stood up, eyes blood-shot, and talking cool as an axe murderer. "This is a rule YOU made," her voice was getting louder.

The preacher sensed this woman wanted a fight, and began to talk over her.

His mother, even more annoyed at this, walked right up to the pulpit and started screaming.

"YOU LET THEM DIP THEY SNUFF. THIS THEY CHURCH. THIS. AIN'T. YO. CHURCH. YOU AIN'T NO GOD!"

The preacher pushed his mother away and, in knee-jerk reaction style, his mother slapped that rat bastard clean across the mouth.

Immediately, ten people in the congregation — some of which were her own siblings — grabbed his mother and yanked her out of the church.

Cool as all hell, she sat on the church steps all of two minutes, put her wig back in place, and marched right back into the church to wait for the post-meeting choir practice. No one dared bother her a second time.

Later that day, mother and son went to Grandmother's house. Grandmother stayed home from the church meeting and her phone was ringing off the hook.

"Gurl, was you down at the church starting with the preacher again?" asked DeShawn's grandmother, agitated to all hell.

"I slapped that bitch in the mouth," DeShawn's mother said coolly as she passed her mother on the way to the bathroom.

DeShawn would eventually learn exactly how much he was like his mother.

• • •

DeShawn didn't remember much of beating Juan's ass. He was later told that he cried, ripped the phone out of the wall, and threw it at Juan's head before screaming, "I have a college degree! I'm better than you!" and jumping over the counter. DeShawn tackled the man, pinned him down, and started punching him in the face.

All DeShawn could recall was being handcuffed and dragged into the police car.

It had all been worth it.

CHAPTER FOUR

DeShawn rolled with a furious crew of fag-gots: Tomas, Leo, and Devin. He was thankful for them.

After he was fired and arrested for beating up his former coworker, he'd called in favors from his homies and was now riding down the Peninsula to Stanford University to some vague new job dealing with sex education and college freshmen, hooked up by Tomas. DeShawn felt a certain way about this gig— he was probably the last goddamn person on Earth that should be lecturing anyone on sexual health. He felt the same way about his friends.

Tomas was one sick fuck. He had been HIV positive since the age of sixteen, when he would use his older brother's ID to sneak into bathhouses and get banged all night. He'd meet men through party lines (an ancient form of telephone hookups where men set up anonymous voicemail accounts and left sketchy details about how and where to find them in public), and get fucked in parks and playgrounds. In his present life, just to be a total fucked-up human being, Tomas would get tested at STD clinics and not tell the nurses he already knew he was positive. The nurse would inform him and he would have a fake panic attack, start crying and throwing things, and fall on the floor and have to be carried out. He did this bullshit just for the sheer fun of it.

Leo was an even sicker fuck. He grew up in some hellhole in rural Kansas. On a recent trip home to his father's funeral, Leo "rekindled" an old "romance" with a man twenty years his senior—the same man that molested him when he was just a kid. Leo was in the passenger seat texting his "ex-boyfriend." DeShawn was grossed out by the whole idea, but he had his own problems.

He was in the backseat relating to Devin— who at twenty-two was the youngest, and coincidently the cleanest, of the crew—his anger over the night before. Young Devin listened raptly to DeShawn bitch, bitch, bitch.

Last night DeShawn had taken a mix of drugs and decided to fulfill a fantasy he'd had for some years—the one where he goes to the back of the sex club, lies down on the floor with a towel over his head, and lets a bunch of gnarly strangers rail him. For *years* DeShawn had searched for the courage to make this dream real, but there were problems with its execution. DeShawn lay on the grimy sex club floor for hours, high and waiting for nothing, his pussy cold and lonely. No one would fuck him. *Am I coming off too desperate?* he asked as he collected what was left of his dignity and left.

Devin giggled and returned to reading his copy of *Vogue*. Devin had come to the crew as a failed experiment of Tomas; they met online somewhere, but when they met in person Tomas understood quickly that he would only ruin the young boy's dreams. So instead they became friends because Devin was just SO. DAMN. CUUUUTE. And extreme.

Devin did shit like insisting on getting tested with all new potential sex partners. DeShawn was baffled by this bullshit; like, *why the fuck would you ever?* He could not move past the conundrums this would impose. What if you found out you had more diseases than your date? Not that it was a competition, but one would certainly be exposed as a whore with reckless judgment. Who the fuck needed this much pressure? And on a *first date* no less? Wasn't life hard enough?

On the inside, though, he envied young

boys like Devin—boys who were smart enough to realize there was something worth protecting. This knowledge had passed by the three other men in the car completely. They had exhausted their risk.

"You keep that pussy of yours clean and find you a real good husband. Don't be like your older brothers here," DeShawn would find himself saying to Devin.

DeShawn was consistent in that he told the same lie to all his potential sex partners: he had previously been in a terrible relationship with some lying whore or another, been scared, and subsequently celibate for the past three months. He noticed that people liked hearing the word "celibate"—it implied "new" or "gently worn," perhaps even "lightweight virginal," and most importantly "not suspect." Or maybe people were just turned on by the fact that someone had hurt him and that he needed rescuing. Nonetheless, DeShawn was older than Devin and past the wide-eyedness of it all. DeShawn, like any jaded bitch in her prime, made it a practice to only get tested with men who bought him dinner first. The rest of those fuckers could eat it.

"The miracles of modern science have made it so that there is a pill for goddamn nearly everything," remarked Tomas. "Why feel guilty?"

"Don't listen to Tomas, Devin. He's gonna burn in hell," said Leo, as he continued messaging his former molester.

• • •

The car arrived in the parking lot of the student medical center and DeShawn was carted off to the waiting room where about seven other educators sat. The room itself was painted a pristine white, with a refrigerator, coffeemaker, computer, and water fountain. On the bulletin board were several dozen flyers for theater shows. As DeShawn understood it, this was a side job for theater people between shows, requiring some performance skills but generally an easy gig.

After gulping unnecessary amounts of coffee, DeShawn was introduced to the team leader who hurriedly greeted him and said, "Come along."

He and his friends disappeared into what seemed like separate medical exam rooms along the same corridor as the waiting room. DeShawn figured the team leader was escorting him to a classroom for his lecture, so he was surprised when he was led into a room occupied by an older white gentleman.

"DeShawn, this is Gary," the team leader said dryly. "You will watch him for your first training." And then he left, just as quickly as he came.

Gary was a cute man. He looked to be in his early sixties, with ice-blue eyes, a big daddy belly, and a seemingly good nature to boot.

"Why do you think you are right for this job?" Gary inquired in what seemed to be a doubtful tone.

DeShawn was slightly offended. "I am the glittering example of emotional, mental, and sexual health," he replied in a "fuck you old dude I don't know" tone that he was sure Gary picked up on.

Surveying the scene, DeShawn noticed that on the exam table were a hospital robe, rubber gloves, and lube. *What's all that for?* thought DeShawn. Just then the door opened and in walked two students in white coats—a black boy with dreads and an Indian woman.

"Where's the rest of the class?" DeShawn was getting uneasy.

Gary disrobed and donned the medical gown. DeShawn's confusion continued to grow; as he understood it, he was supposed to be lecturing a class on sexual health. Now things were taking another turn.

"Hello," Gary addressed the students, "this here is DeShawn, he's in training, so I'll be guiding you in the procedure today."

That's when shit got real weird.

The black kid put his finger in Gary's butt, and gave DeShawn a nervous look as if to say, "I'm a straight guy and this is freaking me out." DeShawn winked at the boy once his finger was fully inserted in Gary. "Okay, now put another finger in," said Gary, and after that, "Now see if you can fit three." Afterward, the boy washed his hands looking completely traumatized. DeShawn doubted the boy's future as a doctor.

When the woman examined Gary's dick for lymph nodes, he got the biggest boner ever, but casually assured the girl, "It's natural."

Even through all this, DeShawn at some point found a way to get bored. He dozed off and started snoring. Gary, midway through getting fingered by yet another premed student, had to stop his exam and wake DeShawn up. He then asked DeShawn to leave the room. He was fired on his first day — a new record for DeShawn.

On the way back to Oakland, DeShawn yelled at Tomas, "Why the fuck didn't you tell me that I was going to get fingered at this job?!"

Tomas replied coolly, "Well, the job description was in the email I sent. Did you read the email?"

DeShawn shut the fuck up because he totally hadn't.

CHAPTER FIVE

Now, back in Alabama for the funeral, DeShawn noticed a distinct shift in power at his old church. DeShawn's mother had become the preacher.

It happened just like this: his mother started to say she was having visions at night. The sweet Lord was calling on her to speak for him.

This all had been brewing for a bit. His mother left the church for a while and joined a Primitive Baptist church on the other side of town. She soon left that church because she thought it was unfair that they didn't allow women to preach. She soon switched back to the Missionary Baptist church she grew up in. "Us Missionary Baptists are very liberal," remarked DeShawn's aunt. He took this explanation with a grain of salt.

There wasn't much in the way of competition for his mother. What had once been a congregation of roughly 120 people some twenty-five years ago, now had dwindled to about thirty. "People are losing hope," his mother said.

For generations the church functioned as theater, concert venue, meeting place, and real-time soap opera. It helped the field people deal with the boredom and futility of their lives. But years of drama had taken its toll on the congregation's faith in the infrastructure. Before her there had been three generations of corrupt preachers. They courted women in the church, bought nice cars with the congregation's money, and were generally annoying fucking people.

Burned forever in his childhood memory was one particular pastor who had the really *fucking* annoying habit of starting every statement in his fireside-revival-style sermons with, "AND MY BIBLE TELLS ME . . ." He would say, "AND MY BIBLE TELLS ME . . . SEEK AND YOU SHALL FIND"; or, "AND MY BIBLE TELLS ME . . . WE WILL BE FREE OF ETERNAL DAMNATION"; or even creepier shit like, "AND MY BIBLE TELLS ME . . . I'VE BEEN WASHED IN THE BLOOD OF THE LAMB."

One particular time the preacher got so gnarly with his pronunciation that he hacked up a huge green loogie that then sat on the corner of his mouth. In his holy fever he tried to wipe it off quickly with a kerchief and ended up smearing it into his beard, where it stayed, faintly iridescent, for the rest of the sermon.

Later that same sermon, some bitch got so drunk on the Holy Spirit that she started screaming, "YAAAAAAAS JESUS," and nearly tossed her baby into the back pew. Luckily, a man caught the toddler. As a child, DeShawn would see this hullabaloo and stick his nose back in the *X-Men* comic hidden inside his Bible. He later figured he learned more about morality in a year of reading *X-Men* comics than he would reading the Bible ten times in a row. This was truth.

He dreamed a lot, and was a slacker. "Why do you move so slow?! You got your head in them books all the time!" was his mother's favorite saying growing up. She threatened to take away all his comic books and the Greek myths he hoarded. She trembled for her son's soul. DeShawn's mother feared his impending homosexuality as if it were a fast-approaching meteor about to hit Earth any second. For a while everyone, even DeShawn's mother, told him that he would be a preacher. The clues were in the way he engaged with people, his high emotional receptivity, and his way with words. All faggots carry these traits early on, and all the adults basically knew DeShawn was a faggot.

Even his appearance was a telltale sign; "Men are going to try to molest you because of your fat ass," his mother often told him. The summer he turned eight, a since long-gone deacon slyly slapped him on the ass while he was ushering. In terms of Christian rhetoric, anything that read as "invitingly feminine" was a danger to be dealt with. It was the same shutdown they gave to Jezebel and to Eve, and now DeShawn's fat ass would have to endure the same tired fuckery. Adults put the idea in his head that he would be a preacher in hopes of killing the mounting rebellion they saw growing in him.

In the years after, when his life was no longer circumscribed by church and the rebellion fully-developed, DeShawn escaped as far as he could: to California. He had sex with Satanists, was wooed by Reiki healers, and even danced naked in the woods on Pagan holidays.

During those same years, his mom would morph, too. There was Sister Pearl, the choir mistress who had given some thirty years of service to the church, but was not allowed to become a mother of the church on a technicality. It was a rule (made by the corrupt former clergy) that in order for a woman to become a mother of the church her husband had to be a deacon. Sister Pearl's husband was the town drunk and a notable whore, leaving her out of the running. Upon DeShawn's mother answering the Lord's call, she lifted the ban and made Sister Pearl a mother of the church. DeShawn cried at her induction ceremony, Sister Pearl dressed all in white, singing in her signature lovely voice.

His mom had eased up on him too. DeShawn's short trip home for his uncle's funeral turned into one month, then two, then three, then more. His mother asked him if he would be the paid church assistant, help with the books, act as secretary at church meetings, and hand out the wine during sacrament.

She offered the position on one condition: that he keep all his pentagram tattoos completely covered and not mention his own "religious proclivities" to anyone in the church. "Most of the congregation is too old to go on the Internet, they don't know anything about you unless you tell them." She side-eyed him.

"I won't, Mama. I promise," said DeShawn, and that was that.

• • •

There had been a lot of fags and dykes in their church growing up; DeShawn recalled a great many of them. His older second cousin once removed always wore white with his hair flat and finger waved in the front and in a beehive in the back. He would politely sit cross-legged in the third pew, extreme left-hand side, with his three children all next to him. He stopped coming after the preacher talked to him about his "lifestyle."

There was Sister Nancy, who was a fuck-head of a Bible school teacher. DeShawn remembered once asking her if a child dies before hearing about Jesus, did that child go to hell? Sister Nancy thought really, really long and hard before she concluded, "Every lamb should have heard of Jesus by now." Even as a young boy, DeShawn knew ol' Sister Nancy wasn't hitting on shit with that response. She was later "talked to" by the preacher for having a baby out of wedlock. Later still, she moved to Kentucky and married some white woman.

Deacon Miles was the youth deacon-in-training who ran off to New Orleans in the late nineties and was dancing for men in strip clubs. Not much more was heard of him until he returned to the church years later. DeShawn could never figure out if Deacon Miles was a fag for real or trade. He always seemed more like trade.

In full Southern Baptist stereotype mode was DeShawn's younger cousin, the choir leader. Sister Pearl had tried to rope DeShawn into being the youth choir leader, but he knew that would be settling for middle management, and — in the eyes of God no less — that had to be some sort of sin. DeShawn briefly considered being the next youth minister prodigy; that's where the real power lay.

DeShawn would prod and poke his beautiful, young choir leader cousin, "Dear, do you ever feel oppressed here?"

The boy looked back at DeShawn strangely, "What does oppressed mean?" It was worse than DeShawn had thought.

Or was it?

The younger cousin had an office job, an apartment with a boyfriend as upwardly mobile as he was, and no general angst. DeShawn thought, *Wait, he's actually happy . . . perhaps*. It had to be a generation gap or something. The thought of only fucking one man was its own unique form of hell; DeShawn understood that he left his mother's home mostly to score dick and try drugs. Reasonable curiosities, but they escaped some people, like DeShawn's cousin. Conversely, this curiosity hit some men in the face. DeShawn thought this might be happening with the new youth minister.

His name was Andre Bosant and DeShawn's mother elected him the new youth minister because she knew his mother. He was not quite sixteen years old, grew up in Louisiana, and had been in and out of juvenile detention centers since he was nine. He cut a fool down in Louisiana so badly that his mom packed up their lives and came to Alabama when he was thirteen. When he was fourteen God started talking to him and wanted Andre to speak for him. The boys' mothers met some two years ago and were quick friends, and that's when DeShawn's mother nominated Andre for youth minister.

Andre was very engaging. He had high emotional receptivity and a way with words. To DeShawn, he seemed like the type of boy that had curiosities; he was perhaps one of the most curious youngsters DeShawn had ever met. Andre had a slight frame and was of average height, a very light-skinned black boy, freckles on his face with reddish brown hair, and hazel eyes like big marbles. In other words, Andre looked like exactly what you would expect from a light-skinned Creole boy named "Andre Bosant."

One day, DeShawn was refilling Bibles in the back pew after Wednesday Bible study when he felt a soft breath on the back of his neck. DeShawn turned around, startled, and saw Andre there, smiling like a pervert with a stack of Bibles in his hand.

"You had a fly on your neck, I blew it off," said Andre.

DeShawn caught on to his game: "Well that's funny Andre, I didn't *feel* a fly land on me."

Andre licked his lips in this certain kind of way. He handed DeShawn the Bibles and their hands touched a moment more than they should have. Their eyes locked for longer than was socially acceptable. Back in the day fags had to look for each other in handshakes and eye contact, so as not to be detected by the general populace. DeShawn knew that it must be something encoded in their DNA, because how else would a young boy have these talents?

The next week DeShawn was weak and decided to meet Andre down at the river at midnight. Andre pulled out a little bottle of whiskey and started crying about how his mom had pushed him into the preacher thing after she found him in bed with a boy in New Orleans. The night got later and DeShawn was pressed against a car, half fighting off Andre's attack kiss, half savoring it. Andre had seen some of DeShawn's nasty movies online. They had turned him on something crazy. The boy pushed up on DeShawn, a hard-on in his pants. DeShawn collected himself. The taboos of the young boy—his judgment was telling him not to cross this line.

He began to think that old Andre Bosant was going to get him in trouble one day.

DeShawn decided he would allow it.

CHAPTER SIX

Dead lovers never go away. This was a theme that kept slapping DeShawn in the face like a five-pound dick, over and over and over again.

He thought about that time he made love to Jatius McClansy, nearly one year before Jatius shot himself in the head.

He had snuck through the cotton field and climbed in Jatius's window. The older boy made DeShawn undress, and, being the younger of the two, he felt a sort of shame for his body. He used his little hands to cover his penis. Jatius got annoyed.

"Well, what gon' happen nigga when you gotta change in PE class in high school? You gon' hide then too?"

DeShawn was visibly humiliated and Jatius backed off a little. He stood up from his bed and pulled down his pants, revealing his erect penis.

"Don't trip, DeShawn. One day yours'll be

this big," he said, grabbing DeShawn's hand and putting it on his penis.

He lied to me, thought DeShawn, whose mind switched back to the present as he rested on his back in his mother's front yard.

The heat wasn't oppressive today. DeShawn was babysitting his nephew, who was chasing butterflies in the sunflower garden. DeShawn only allowed himself to daydream a second or two: he was not in a gutter looking at the stars; he was in a pillowy field of grass staring at the swift moving clouds. As it was for all day-dreamers, a second or two of indulgence could fuel a whole chapter in a book. He looked at the eastern sky and saw a cloud that reminded him of a penis and thought about his new lover, Andre. Andre was going to be sixteen years old next week. A feeling of annoyance came over him. Andre fucked like a teenager who watched *way* too much fucking porn. DeShawn remembered looking at the boy's face during sex last night; Andre was giving him a blow job and making these distorted, silly faces, as if performing for a camera that wasn't there. Andre grew up in a world where porn could be accessed by a few keystrokes on a computer. DeShawn came from a world where porn had to be discreetly stolen from his parents' closet at some undetectable hour of the night. He remembered pressing the play button on the VCR with just enough pressure to deaden the inevitable loud *click* that set the machine into motion, careful not to wake up his mother. This new generation had it way too fucking easy, and they were clearly paying the price for it.

Sex with the teenager was all he had here. He missed California and the bathhouse, the place he called home.

He sighed and stretched as he thought of the catalog of memories he collected there. His body grew warm with a familiar tingle. DeShawn forgave Andre for being a sorta bad lay; he felt sorry for the boy, all tucked away like a prisoner in this Bible Belt hell. DeShawn was only slightly older than Andre when he ran away to California and got his first experience of what several men at a time tasted like.

He remembered that first night he got high and drunk and went to the bathhouse and stayed all night; he couldn't have been more than nineteen. All the men had worked him over real good. He was scared at the time, but now remembered it fondly. Then his troubles came.

It was one night some thirteen years after his introduction to the baths, to be exact. He looked in the mirror and his hair was prematurely graying. He surmised it was a mix of genetics and too much experience that bred a certain weariness in him. He noticed that all the tops he fucked in his youth were becoming older themselves. He watched his part-time lovers age and not get erections anymore. He didn't want to throw these men away—they had taught him how to fuck well. Maybe one day his dick also wouldn't work the same, which on one level was fine with him—he had certainly put some mileage on that fucker. Either way, some nights at the baths now were spent cuddling with old lovers. This was a different kind of pleasure. These changes were his current-day dilemmas, but then there was the immediate past.

DeShawn walked the halls of the baths so much that he knew his ghost would haunt it one day. His friends would say things like, "Well, you're getting older, you should stop this behavior," or, "Your lifestyle is unhealthy, why not find a man and settle down?"

"Let's say any boy who didn't know what love was walked in a bathhouse high and drunk and got fucked by ten different guys in one night. Could anyone ever settle down and be happy with one man after that much stimulation, that young?" he once heard another slut ask. DeShawn knew that anything was possible, but of course he had his doubts—big ones. On occasion he would still go and see men (some two and a half times his age) walking the halls of the bathhouse endlessly, flashing flaccid cocks, and smiling, no less.

DeShawn once briefly worked at the baths. One night he was cleaning the bathrooms when he heard a meek cry for help from one of the stalls. He saw beneath the stall door a pair of feet moving precariously on the wet, tiled floor. DeShawn cracked the door open and saw a man, he looked to be in his seventies or maybe even eighties, barefoot in a towel. He was so stiff he couldn't gain control of his feet, and DeShawn had to lend a hand to ground him and lead him out of the stall, as a fall at his age could prove fatal. DeShawn looked at the man and all he saw was his future.

Why not find a man and settle down? The thought played on repeat until he heard his nephew cry. DeShawn ran over to the toddler, and the young boy cried, "Bee!" He had been stung.

DeShawn grabbed the baby and went into the house, looking for something to bring comfort. He attended to his brother's child on a sort of autopilot as his mind returned to its previous bullshit.

But what is love? he thought. *It has to be . . .* He couldn't think of anything.

He applied ointment to the child's red and swollen arm, held him close to his chest, and bounced him lightly.

It seemed hard for DeShawn, this idea of structuring his life around some hypothetical Prince Charming that may or may not come; he felt like some dubious Christian waiting for Jesus to return.

Maybe he was too far gone; maybe he didn't really give a shit or maybe he was too brainwashed by feminism. Regardless, the acute boredom of the variables of whatever fictional monogamy he placed himself in washed over him and wrapped around his psyche like a goddamn straitjacket.

He could say he hated the bathhouse — this was true enough — but the opposite seemed like a prison sentence. The thought of his hypothetical monogamous boyfriend slugging into the apartment after work night after night, year after year, both him and this hypothetical man wearing their domestic pajamas, watching movies or reading books to avoid the fact that there was nothing to say — DeShawn felt it was a different kind of loneliness, and one he didn't need. He was already in love with his own kind.

DeShawn's nephew had finally quieted down and was hugging him. He squeezed him back.

Maybe I'm not actually lonely at all.

CHAPTER SEVEN

If DeShawn's life were a movie, the opening shot would be of seven little black bodies (him and his cousins) running through a lush green yard, past bushels of marigolds and sunflowers, playing freeze tag or hide-and-go-seek among the beanstalks in his grandmother's yard.

Perhaps it could be followed by a shot of ten little black bodies (himself, his cousins, his two youngest uncles, one being the dead one) walking the gravel roads, the oldest among them no more than thirteen or fourteen years old.

He thought about his nephew sleeping in the back room of his grandmother's house, and his second cousins playing in the yard. These children went to day care, something unheard of when DeShawn was a field rat running through the cotton with his cousins.

These new children had perhaps not spent

more than twenty minutes outside of the confines of adult supervision. It was a lack of adult supervision that characterized DeShawn's upbringing, and this revealed itself in adulthood in some not-so-surprising ways, namely a resistance to supervision, particularly over himself. He tried to get out of his head about it.

He thought about memory and time and how some years can all run together into one giant stream.

DeShawn was just old enough to pinpoint when the No Shoes, No Shirts, No Service signs started going up at grocery stores all around northern Alabama: it was some time around the late eighties. DeShawn's childhood was defined by going nearly everywhere barefoot; he remembered going with his youngest aunt (in her teens) to the Piggly Wiggly to buy Oreos and they were both barefoot.

DeShawn had six aunts and five uncles. None of them he referred to by name, they were all simply "Uncle" or "Auntie." His uncle who died was the next youngest to DeShawn's youngest aunt, who babysat him the most. One day there was a fight over who would use the one car that was shared among all the youth in the house. DeShawn watched Uncle drag the youngest aunt out of the car by her hair and punch her in the face. DeShawn's aunt, not to be outdone, uppercut his uncle in the stomach, causing him to crouch on his knees in the brown gravel road, where she proceeded to kick him in the head until he bum-rushed her from the ground. More of a struggle ensued: she broke free and he chased her around the house; being much faster than him, she ran the full circumference of the place and caught up to him while his back was turned. She did a running, twenty-foot-long, WWE-style drop-kick that landed on the back of his head and he was down for the count. DeShawn's aunt then took him to Piggly Wiggly to buy Oreos and pick up a girlfriend of hers, and then they all took the car to the river. She cut the arms off his little baby shirt, and he watched as his aunt and her girlfriend picked up boys, making mental notes.

DeShawn chuckled at this recollection. Reclining at his grandmother's house after church, he looked across the room at his maternal grandmother. He saw the tired look in Granny's eyes. It was the look of a woman who had been raising children for three god-damn generations. Her children, her children's children, and now her great-grands were infesting the house like little roaches. "Well goddamn, Grammy, when you gon' retire, girl?!" DeShawn poked at her.

"Shit, man, I guess never," she chuckled

under a deadpan expression. She'd had this dry sense of humor for as long as he could remember. He went to the back room to check on his sleeping nephew; he was still out cold and had been that way since the church service. He went outside to check on his smaller second cousins playing church on the front porch, singing "This Little Light of Mine" together.

Well, I don't like this Christian business one bit, but at least they're having fun, DeShawn thought.

Some twenty-five years ago he sat on those same steps and did the same thing. Cousin so-and-so would preach and wear a sheet as a robe. He prefaced every sentence with, "And my Bible tells me . . . ," just like the annoying preacher at the church. Then he would get the spirit, throw off his robe, and the "congregation" (whatever cousins were around) would fan him, get him some water, help him back into his robe, and carry him back to the pulpit. His cousins were enacting the same game as if it were coded in their goddamn DNA. *Nothing changes*, DeShawn thought.

He scanned the yard—past his grandfather's broken down '67 Dodge truck, and past the marigolds and sunflowers in his grandmother's garden.

A dead kitten was found past the flower

garden when DeShawn was five, and he was accused of killing it, as he was seen in the yard earlier that day with a baseball bat. His grandfather was somewhat of a dramatist, and when DeShawn or any of his cousins did anything bad, he set up a mock court in the living room, with a jury consisting of whatever peers and adults were on hand. This time five cousins and his youngest aunt and uncle were the jury. At five years old he had to plead his case to a jury that didn't believe him. "It had to be you," they kept telling him. By the end of the trial he really believed he'd killed that kitten. The jury unanimously found him guilty. His mother was fond of the saying "Truth crushed to earth will rise again," and sure enough, at a family Christmas dinner many years later, a drunk cousin of his (out of fucking nowhere) casually remarked, mid-dinner *and laughing*, "You know, it was actually me who killed that cat."

· · ·

DeShawn was constantly pulled back into stories like this. He knew his grandmother's face so well; there was history and memory running through it. Whatever was in her was in him. This was how lineage worked.

DeShawn had known some things.

He knew his maternal great-great-grand-mother. He remembered kissing her on the cheek once, and her remarking that he was a "sweet boy"; she was nearing one hundred and had been bedridden for years at that point. DeShawn's mother knew a different woman, a woman who, in her youth, had cleared acres of tree stumps and farmed the land once it was cleared.

He had heard his mother's version of the family's history often, and how he, DeShawn, had indirectly come into being.

DeShawn's great-great-grandmother's parents were born slaves in Virginia—how they got to Alabama was anybody's guess—and they had his great-great-nan who in turn had five children. One of her kids, Earnestine (DeShawn's great-grandmother, whom DeShawn's mother was named after) turned fifteen and became a servant in the house of a local bluesman, Hard Rock Jones. Hard Rock didn't like field work too much, so he learned to play guitar and played the blues along the Chitlin Circuit on up to Chicago and back. Hard Rock had a wife and two kids when he impregnated DeShawn's future great-grand-mother, the aforementioned servant girl, who then gave birth to DeShawn's nan. His grand-mother was raised in a house with only her mother and grandmother and had no contact with her father or her father's side of the family for some thirty-odd years, until one day her half brother came speeding into the cotton field in a Cadillac. He had moved to California in the sixties, and by the seventies was co-owner of a blues club in Oakland, the same club DeShawn would live four blocks away from some thirty years after that.

DeShawn's mother often reminded him, in times of stress, that he came from strong women and therefore could never fail. He thought about their lives, his great- and great-great-nans, as single women in the forties on that little patch of grass in the cotton field, fending off winters, fresh men, and cheats. It was said that people from up north would travel through the South and sell bunk insurance to poor blacks; the women soon learned to never give their money away to anyone.

DeShawn looked at his grandmother's face and understood it as his own.

He looked past the yard with his younger cousins playing church. He looked past the sunflowers and marigolds, the cotton field, the memories of dead kittens, and memory itself. This was Alabama. It shook him a bit. It was the first time in his life that he ever recalled this place feeling like home.

CHAPTER EIGHT

In DeShawn's life there was another death of grave importance. DeShawn flipped through a dusty photo album, so old it still had that adhesive cellophane sheet on top.

There was a picture of a young man from the early seventies, sitting on a black Cadillac parked on a brown gravel road somewhere in rural Arkansas. The man was very handsome, dark skinned, smiling brighter than the sun, wearing bell-bottoms, a white T-shirt with rolled-up sleeves, and a denim newsboy cap that matched the bell-bottoms. He was on his way to the army. That young man, DeShawn's future stepfather, was Big Daddy.

DeShawn was now a good deal older than the boy in that picture. The thought made him shudder inside.

His mother had not been married to Big Daddy very long—just four years, divorcing when DeShawn was eight. The marriage was short, yet felt like an eternity. Violent. It would mark DeShawn the rest of his life. It also produced DeShawn's little brother.

It was hot the day DeShawn, his younger brother, Carl, and his nephew, William, all drove up the highway in Carl's air-conditioned car to make it to the veteran's cemetery to put flowers on Big Daddy's grave.

DeShawn looked at Carl with the same envy with which he always had. DeShawn's biological father flew the coop when he was two, leaving him in the care of his mother, who met his stepfather a short bit afterward. DeShawn always wondered how much of that house's trouble Carl remembered; DeShawn was sure he was too young to remember much of it. Carl's father paid all the bills, leaving DeShawn to feel like a ward of his mother. He grew up feeling like he never had a real say in anything; he was just sort of this appendage that would shrink away to avoid conflict. DeShawn also wondered if Carl remembered him sneaking out of the house to meet Jatius McClansy at night, leaving Carl alone in his little bed.

Ignorance is surely bliss. Carl did not seem to have DeShawn's maladjusted tendencies, and he was sure his younger brother's age and status as the biological son of Big Daddy, the alpha male of the house, had protected him from the evil. It also helped that his stepfather wasn't jealous of Carl.

DeShawn's mother would often tell him Big Daddy would say shit like, "I'm jealous of DeShawn — I always wanted a young mother." Big Daddy's mother had abandoned him. When Big Daddy waltzed into DeShawn and his mother's life, the two were living in the projects. All the older man saw was a single woman and a little boy, and when he looked at the little boy, all he saw was himself. It was a situation he wanted to solve. Problem was, the older man had not checked all of his problems first, and this is how it all got blown to hell. It was a fucked-up (though perhaps common) situation of a young boy competing for the attention of his mother with an older man who never really had one.

"You always paying more attention to that boy than me," Big Daddy would say. He made DeShawn pay a hard price for what he saw as the boy's "privilege."

Big Daddy grew up in Arkansas, the oldest of four boys, each with different dads. His father was a womanizer with a whole nother family altogether. One day, Big Daddy's father moved to California with his other family, leaving lil' Big Daddy behind. Later that year his mother took all of Big Daddy's brothers to

Chicago, and left him behind because he had the darkest skin.

Big Daddy was raised by his maternal aunt, Josephine, a Rosie the Riveter woman—she had worked in the Oakland shipyards in the forties before coming back to Arkansas in the late fifties to buy land and build a farm.

DeShawn had seen the black-and-white pictures of Big Daddy and his Aunt Jo in the yard together. In one, Big Daddy was playing with some baby chickens and his Aunt Jo was patting the young boy on the head. This picture always made DeShawn cry because he saw Big Daddy as a child and knew how his life ended. Big Daddy had started off like DeShawn, an innocent little boy who was about to have the world descend upon him.

Big Daddy did what every man of his generation who wanted to leave the Delta did— he joined the military. There were mountains of pictures from his military days. Big Daddy as a young man in Korea, Germany, Panama, and other places a boy from Arkansas probably never expected himself to be.

DeShawn had known much about the black body versus the prison industrial complex, but no one ever seemed to talk about the military industrial complex and the lives it rearranged—not always for the better. DeShawn thought too long and too often about a young

Big Daddy, just shy of twenty, a young man with no father figure to speak of being raised by captains and sergeants. It was frightening.

His stepfather would sometimes tell the story of a bunk partner from basic training, some white boy from the Ozarks who would look at him like he was a ghost. Big Daddy asked the young man what the problem was, to which he remarked, "Man, I ain't being funny, but I just done ain't never seen no colored man before." Big Daddy would laugh his ass off every time he told this story.

But these were all things DeShawn learned later. There were still the first, vivid memories of Big Daddy, the ones DeShawn couldn't unsee.

DeShawn and his mother moved into Big Daddy's house. That had been a mistake from day damn one. DeShawn's earliest memory was of being awoken by a fight, lots of screaming and things crashing about. Barely five, young DeShawn walked past the bathroom and saw his mother's clothes on the floor, soaking wet. He slowly walked into the living room of the tiny apartment and saw his stepfather in his underwear, hitting his mother in the face and tossing her out the front door in only her underwear.

DeShawn's soul saw this and went on a journey inside of itself; he held on to the feeling for life — hate. He hated Big Daddy. It would be the first of many such scenes to play out in front of the young boy for years and years.

"The only reason you're here is because I feel like being nice to you," Big Daddy would say. Or, "You think I'm low down, boy? What about your father who sits his ass in southern Alabama and leaves me to take care of you?"

DeShawn fought back the only way he could: he stayed quiet. He learned that the only way to beat an enemy bigger than you is to survive them. It's hard. It warps the soul. But it is a strategy, and the only one for a boy who could not fight back. Big Daddy was the first of a hundred men DeShawn felt he had no power over, who were merely obstacles to be survived. He felt tired of just surviving all the time.

Every time he had a fight with DeShawn's mother, the man's favorite trick to quiet the house was to sit in the back room for hours and clean his guns. DeShawn remembered walking on eggshells, his heart palpitating. He could hear the guns clicking all through the house. With each click his little heart would stop. *Is this man going to kill us?* That day of carnage never came, though; the only person Big Daddy would kill was himself.

• • •

DeShawn grew up one day, same way all lit-tle boys do. His mom had long since divorced Big Daddy, but DeShawn, just shy of eighteen, had escaped to California, putting as much distance as possible between himself and his childhood home. To go any farther you had to start swimming.

DeShawn had not been five months in the sunny state before he got a frantic call; it was early March and he was stoned in the punk warehouse where he was living. His mother was on the other end: "Big Daddy is dead, baby. You have to come home."

During his time in the army Big Daddy had picked up a hellified coke problem, which at its crescendo turned to crack. DeShawn didn't know his stepfather was addicted to crack his entire childhood, but this explained a lot. Why the man was so goddamn erratic all the time; why, even though he had a decent-paying job, violent fights about money dom-inated the household. The dead man main-tained a desk job some thirty-plus years while nursing a crack cocaine addiction. Years down the line, DeShawn himself would learn the particular dance of being a high-functioning substance abuser.

They found Big Daddy's body next to his bed. He had been smoking crack, and a blood vessel in his neck clogged and exploded. There was a spray of blood on the wall where he fell. He was fifty-two.

DeShawn remembered watching Big Daddy's parents — two people in their late sixties — get into an argument and almost come to blows some five feet away from their dead son's body while the preacher was reciting the burial rites. They had to be separated. He began to understand the hell that was Big Daddy's life.

• • •

DeShawn stood six feet above what was left of the man he knew to be his father. It was his job to make sure whatever it was that killed Big Daddy on the inside would not be passed on to his nephew. That was the charge of the living.

DeShawn looked at Carl raising William by himself. William's mother was a heroin addict and in jail. Much like their mother before them, DeShawn and his brother loved drug addicts and other forms of dubious company.

Despite his reluctance to do so, DeShawn eventually came to peace with Big Daddy. This man who lived a short, bitter, intense, uneven, and unfair life. DeShawn could not help but tear up about it from time to time — on buses, in the middle of class, sometimes while talking to people. There was nothing that he wouldn't give for one last conversation with Big Daddy. He left flowers on the grave and retreated to the car with his brother and nephew.

DeShawn remembered Big Daddy's prophetic words to him: "One day, when you're a man, you'll understand what I'm mad about, boy."

This much became true—a lot truer than DeShawn was ready for.

CHAPTER NINE

Lately, DeShawn's thoughts were haunted by dead lovers and, strangely enough, polar bears. The night before, his mother confirmed a memory DeShawn thought he made up.

Every summer young DeShawn would drive with his mother and cousins to Birmingham. They would always visit the church where the four little black girls died in a bombing, and then go to the zoo to see the polar bears. In *July*.

"Mama," asked DeShawn, very inquisitively, "Would we really see polar bears, in *Alabama*, in *July*?"

"Yes, baby! You used to love the polar bears," she said, three seconds before the epiphany struck. "Wait a minute, you're right! That's *fucked-up*! Oh, those poor bears!"

There were always harder truths to dig through. DeShawn also didn't trust his memory of the man in the pink suit.

His mother's older sister and her teenage daughter lived up the way; they were his caretakers. When DeShawn rifled through his earliest memories, the man with a pink suit was always in the background. He was an older black man and had on sunglasses, a pink suit, and a fedora. In the boy's mind he looked like Panama Jack from the shirts that were popular in the eighties. The man walked with a cane, and his aunt and cousin didn't mumble a word to him. DeShawn's memory of the man's specter-like presence creeped him the fuck out, and he finally asked his great aunt about the man. "Oh, that was Arnold Jackson," she explained in a kind of cool voice. "We never talked to him because he was a rapist and a child molester. He attacked some girls in the neighborhood and was after your cousin for years." His aunt spoke in a surprisingly disinterested, matter-of-fact tone as she continued crocheting.

"Some ghosts are real," DeShawn said to himself as he pushed along the highway.

• • •

As assistant to his mother the preacher, DeShawn cleaned the church, washed the choir robes, and took care of all the necessaries. Today he had to go to Blood of the Lamb

Bible Supply in Cullman to pick up the programs for next Sunday. He hated driving to Cullman—it was Ku Klux Klan territory. As a boy, he remembered seeing "I Ride with Nathan" stickers (referring to Nathan Bedford, the first Grand Wizard of the KKK) with the text printed over Confederate flags.

DeShawn watched the news at night and saw black churches were burning down all over the place, the latest one just some three hours away from his church. He didn't like that all the local black churches were registered at the Bible supply in Klansville—he didn't want them knowing their whereabouts—but then again, they had the cheapest stationery and the next Bible supply was all the way in Birmingham, so he closed his eyes, mouth, and ears to all evil and went on to Cullman.

He stared very hard at the stationery options; he couldn't decide if he wanted the programs printed with doves or sacred crosses. He went with the doves—the crosses seemed too literal. On his way to the checkout he turned left at the candle aisle and saw something that nearly shook him out of his bones: Skylar goddamn Prescott, plain as day and not looking at all different than he did as a teenager. Skylar was curiously examining the Jesus figurines.

DeShawn stopped just short of a panic attack, and he ducked into the next aisle to collect himself before making a beeline for the front door. He started his car and gassed away as fast as he could. The memory choked him the same way Skylar did that one summer.

If he had to think about it — like, really think about it — Skylar was the predecessor to Arnold, the dead white boy DeShawn loved. The main difference was that Arnold, when confronted with the mortal coil of life, did what a lot of sensitive people do, and committed suicide. Skylar, however, did what most assholes do: become a born-again Christian. Of all the white, rock-and-roll-boy dick DeShawn had tasted, he couldn't think of anyone in that subcategory he despised more than Skylar Prescott.

DeShawn met Skylar as a teenager when DeShawn was fifteen and was working at a surf-and-turf restaurant by the highway. He was the only black boy working there and was weird. He was 270 pounds, with a high-pitched, musical, girly voice and weird nerd glasses he copped because of his obsession with Rivers Cuomo from Weezer. Needless to say, his midnineties, rural Alabama town didn't get it. They mostly pretended not to see him; he would bus tables and take plates from customers as if he were a ghost, the clientele seeming to stare right through him. The boss's wife was always there to offer up a pep talk:

"Why, you're the fastest and most handsome bus boy we've ever had!" she would say in this sweeping way, and DeShawn would smile gratefully and work harder. He was young still, and had not built an adequate enough bullshit detector.

After a couple of months, DeShawn got the notion he wanted to wait tables, and asked the boss's wife if he could. She said he couldn't because he was too young and they didn't hire male waiters anymore because the one they hired years ago was a gay man (who the boss imitated by lisping and prancing around), and his employment went over like a lead balloon. DeShawn accepted that it wasn't meant to be, until the day Skylar showed up. Skylar was also fifteen, but skinny, with a deep voice, and white. It took DeShawn another couple of years to figure out why Skylar got to be a waiter and he didn't.

Skylar and DeShawn bonded over both being devotees of *Alternative Nation* on MTV and playing punk music. Skylar even rolled DeShawn's first joint. One New Year's Eve Skylar convinced DeShawn to skip church so they could go see a ska band that was performing up the road. DeShawn was captivated by the show — the band members were dressed as mummies and throwing cake and spaghetti everywhere — when he felt a tap on the back of his shoulder. DeShawn's mother was standing behind him in a wig and sunglasses. "Your grandmother is in the hospital. We have to go." As he later found out, DeShawn's mother was lying, and drove him straight to the New Year's Eve gathering at church, where he sat right next to his grandmother, sulking.

• • •

Skylar was an only child with divorced parents; his father was a professor and his mother a furniture dealer who'd previously been a cook. DeShawn quickly noted how different Skylar's parents were from his own. They would quit talking whenever Skylar screamed, "Shut the fuck up!" and they also sent him to shrinks to put him on medication for his disorders. DeShawn's parents, when they weren't threatening him, mostly just ignored him. He eventually figured that's why he hated Skylar. When Skylar was a depressed teenager the world came running, but when DeShawn was depressed no one gave a shit.

Skylar's mother was particularly baffling to DeShawn. The first night he came over to Skylar's house he noticed all the super-old furniture and figurines. Apparently the style was art deco, as he would later learn. Skylar's mother eventually came home black-out wasted with a friend. She looked at DeShawn and said to her friend, "Look, a handsome black man. I want him to lick my pussy." She lifted her skirt and exposed her pantyless, shaved vagina to DeShawn. Skylar hit the wall and started yelling, and his mother fell down. DeShawn was delighted. He had never seen anybody's mom that wasted *or* a vagina. He liked Skylar's mom.

DeShawn started hanging out at Skylar's house more and more. His mother would cook French cuisine and let the boys drink wine. Skylar's mother only had gay male friends, and so the two boys would dine in the company of all of the town's drunken posh gay dudes. Sometimes they would hit on DeShawn, and a tingly feeling would run through him.

One night after Skylar and DeShawn finished band practice in Skylar's basement, Skylar reached over for DeShawn's dick, which stiffened immediately. Skylar pulled it out of DeShawn's vintage trousers and fell to his knees, sucking as if he were attempting to drain DeShawn's soul. "Come in my mouth," Skylar said, breath heavy and red in the face. DeShawn let it rip. The two made it upstairs to the bedroom, where Skylar put on a porn movie. It was a cheesy one with some skinny blond woman in lingerie getting choked by the guy fucking her. Skylar put DeShawn on his stomach facing the porn movie, licked his finger, and stabbed it into DeShawn's anus; DeShawn winced.

Skylar had talked about how he got fucked when he was twelve by this older boy in the neighborhood, and that he had wanted to try it again. Apparently, this would be the night. He spit a huge wad of saliva onto DeShawn's butthole, aimed his hard dick, and thrust it into DeShawn full throttle. A lightning bolt of pain shot through DeShawn so hard he felt nauseous, but the feeling was overtaken by adrenaline once he realized he was getting fucked for the first time. Skylar wrapped his hand around DeShawn's throat and began to choke him, mimicking the porn. DeShawn was crippled by stimulation. Before he could register all of the feelings he was having, Skylar let out a deep gasp, his dick frozen and pulsating inside DeShawn, and collapsed on top of him, sweating and breathing hard. DeShawn put together a sentence in his head: *I just lost my virginity.*

Skylar and DeShawn continued on like this for some year and a half before Skylar started dating girls and ignoring DeShawn's phone calls. The two would have sex one last time four years later, after DeShawn had escaped the clutches of Alabama and settled in some sleepy Midwestern college town a month or two before moving to California. Skylar's touring band was passing through, and the two fucked on a pile of dirty laundry in DeShawn's room.

The years passed, and Skylar became more and more of a Christian. DeShawn figured he was rebelling against his too-liberal upbringing. Skylar began posting shit online about God, and how he was happy that he had found faith in the Almighty, and had a wife who obeyed him. Sometime after that, Skylar became a preacher at some snotty white church near the highway.

DeShawn pulled away from Blood of the Lamb Bible Supply feeling like he dodged a goddamn bullet. It probably wouldn't have been the worst to exchange an awkward hello with Skylar, but on this day he just didn't have it in him. DeShawn tapped the accelerator on his mom's old Camaro and flung his little being up the highway, thinking about how some men were dead and buried, and other men were not, but the memory of them seemed just as buried and far away.

CHAPTER TEN

DeShawn was exhausted.

He was lying on a couch in his grand-mother's living room that was positioned directly under the air conditioner. It was also his favorite spot in childhood.

He was in a postchurch haze. He had attended morning service, and then a second service at a neighboring church, followed by dinner. To him, it was some sort of magic watching all the little old black women in two-ton church hats walking into the back of the church with covered dishes of fried chicken, fried catfish, roasted ham, barbecued beef, green beans, mac and cheese, corn, yams (the only side dish that didn't have some form of pork in them), and carbs, dear goddess, all the carbs. There were biscuits with butter, cornbread muffins, pies, cobblers, and eight different kinds of cakes. He sampled every dish *twice*.

DeShawn sat in a stupor and wondered why in fact he didn't have diabetes yet (he had raged on this type of Sunday soul-food suicide binge since childhood), but thought it best to not provoke the gods by asking about his impending illnesses. "Maybe I'll get away with it for a couple more years," he said as he slumped off of the couch to get a much-needed glass of water. It impressed him how food hangovers worked, that a meal could cause a hangover that was just as paralyzing as one from drugs or drink. It was fascinating.

He looked out of the back window of his grandmother's kitchenette, sipping his cool lemon water slowly. He was amazed at the ruse he constructed. While at the second church program, shaking the congregation's hands with his mother, all he had to say was, "Preacher _____ is my mother," and people would hug him and shake his hand harder. It blew him away that all he had to do was wear a suit and a smile, and not one member of the church could begin to guess that he was a raging slut. He almost felt pure again, or maybe just got comfortable with the idea that, even as a raging slut, people should respect him like this all the time. *I could get used to this*, DeShawn thought, taking a sip of water.

At church that day, just as DeShawn's mind (inevitably) switched from his newfound purity back to sex, he saw a familiar girl walk up to him after the service. Her name was Vickie Sue Thomas, she was two grades ahead of him in school and basically a sweet girl.

"DESHAWN!!!! HOW YOU DOIN' BABY BOY?!?!" she squealed as she vigorously hugged him.

DeShawn was fond of Vicki. She was cut a pretty raw deal early on in middle school. DeShawn had been in the fifth grade and Vicki in the seventh, the summer she sucked DeShawn's older cousin's dick and got branded a slut. She was basically shunned, and for the rest of the year Vicki would bring a Bible and a highlighter with her on the bus and sit quietly and highlight passages. "It gives me strength somehow," she would say.

In the years to follow, DeShawn would understand how truly fucked-up and sad that story was—not just because of the patriarchy, but also because in seventh grade Vicki still only read at a fourth-grade level. She for sure didn't understand what she was highlighting. The other day, DeShawn, being somewhat well-read, picked up a Bible for shits and giggles, and could only shake his head at how he basically didn't know what the fuck it was talking about.

Either way, it was nice to see Vicki and he even got a ride back to Grandma's with her after church.

• • •

He was at his grandmother's alone now — not the rarest occurrence, but one that as long as he could remember always inspired only one idea: jerking off.

Everything DeShawn learned offhand about sex happened at his grandmother's house. His grandfather was a huge porn fiend and kept porno magazines and movies in every nook and cranny of the house, and DeShawn had a shit-ton of older cousins who had no problem sharing the bounty of XXX artifacts found virtually everywhere. DeShawn reasoned that he had seen his first hardcore porn movie by the time he was five — quite possibly before. One time he remembered a group of his cousins, younger uncles, and neighborhood boys all gathered in the den watching porn on VHS, and his grandmother walking in on them. There was no reaction on her face; she didn't even raise her voice. She simply walked to the VHS player, turned it off, and took the tape with her saying plainly, "Remember that the people on this tape are *actors*." DeShawn — in his present — understood his grandmother's cool angst. There were the times his grandfather would stumble home wasted and watch porn in the living room, and the matron would have to collect all the grandbabies and hold them in the back of the house so they wouldn't witness it. "He's watching his naked soap operas again," she would say.

It was also at his grandmother's that DeShawn jacked off to completion for the first time.

It was after church one Sunday and his mother, grandmother, aunt, and brother went to get barbecue. He stayed at his grandmother's, and soon went riffling through a box of porn in his grandparents' closet. Inside he found a 1986 *Penthouse Forum*. It contained a few pictures, but it was mostly text on worn pink paper. That issue's "Letter of the Month" contained a story about a bisexual man who lived somewhere in California and wrote about a tryst he and his girlfriend were having with a male neighbor.

In one scene, it described the two men, one blond and the other dark haired, jacking each other off and eventually fucking on the beach. Years later, DeShawn wondered how this had altered his mental landscape — that is, reading about gay sex as opposed to seeing it in porn. He had his tryst with Jatius, of course, but he never ejaculated. It was time now.

He read over and over the one paragraph about how the two men were on the beach, and the blond man was jacking off for the dark-haired man, and when he came it shot clear past the dark-haired man's head. One sentence described how the blond man stroking his own shaft, slowly, fully, and repeatedly, made the dark-haired man get off. *I should try that*, thought DeShawn.

He went to the bathroom and took off his pants, but kept on his sweater. He lay on his back on the bathroom floor, got himself hard, and worked himself over the way he had read about in the magazine. His nerves felt tingly, and he lay there doing this for what seemed like an eternity. *Is it supposed to take this long?* he wondered. He kept at it for what seemed like another, even longer, eternity until *boom, pop*, and fireworks exploded. He felt the spillage on his hands. It was like a silent epiphany, that moment of *oh shit, I get it!*

DeShawn could still remember that flush of feeling and the story from the book. He was aroused now.

He went to his grandmother's bathroom, took off his pants, and left on his Sunday shirt. He lay on his back on the bathroom floor and started jerking off.

CHAPTER ELEVEN

DeShawn's mother hated her mother. It was a problem. DeShawn's grandmother didn't like her daughter much either. This certainly compounded the problem.

He couldn't blame either of them for the rift. As DeShawn's mother would often explain: "I was the third daughter. I was third and female. Your grandmother wanted a boy. That bitch always made me pay for not being a boy." DeShawn believed his mother when she said this. People often called his mom "crazy" or "hysterical," but DeShawn believed his mom to be a psychic and a prophet when it came to dealing with people. All the "crazy" shit she predicted always had a way of coming true — never at the time — but always eventually.

DeShawn's grandmother was a different story. She had a quiet wisdom. She was also generally right too. DeShawn was her favorite grandchild. He couldn't tell if it was 'cause he was a boy or 'cause he played rock and roll just like her brother and father. Maybe it was because he was the lead male soloist in the children's choir, or maybe because out of thirty grandchildren, he was the first and youngest to be baptized. Regardless of why, she loved DeShawn the same way his mom loved his great-great-grandmother. (His grandmother hated her own mother—it was a trait that skipped generations it seemed.)

DeShawn's mother would say shit like, "Your grandmother was a baby factory. She was a slave to Granddad. She never stood up for herself." But all DeShawn could see when he looked at his grandmother was a woman who didn't have many choices. She lived in the rural South, the bastard child of a traveling blues musician, and started having babies in the fifties. DeShawn's grandmother had three babies by his grandfather before he even married her. All DeShawn could say to his mother was "Dear god, Mama can we PLEASE be nice to Grandma?! Wasn't her life, like, hard?"

Meanwhile, DeShawn's grandmother couldn't deal with her daughter's fierceness. "I'm gon' beat that bitch's ass if she roll up here one more Sunday starting shit with me," Granny said very matter-of-fact from her rocking chair on the front porch as she spotted DeShawn's mother's car come up the road.

And there were other points to note. DeShawn's grandmother gave birth to fourteen children (two died at birth), and DeShawn thought it was cold for his mom to call a woman who had spent 126 months of her life pregnant, before rural women had access to birth control, a "baby factory." DeShawn also saw it as fact that if you have that many fucking kids, you're bound to hate some of them. Like, who the fuck can love a dozen maniacs *all* the time? He saw a mother-daughter feud that wasn't going anywhere. DeShawn also knew that he and his mother were just alike. Her constant emotional flashing on *her* mother was a way to get her needs met. With eleven siblings, one finds a way to get attention — good or bad.

DeShawn *loved* Grandma. She was a pretty solid badass. He remembered the first job she had in the late eighties. It was up the road in Athens, Alabama, at a factory called ConAgra, a chicken processing plant. She would ride with the other single woman her age that lived up the road. DeShawn was young when she had that job, but as an adult he was keen on how strong it must have made her feel. Shitty job as it was, it was the first time in almost thirty-five years of raising children that she finally had her own income. But, even then, his grandmother had to answer to the patriarchal backlash in another cruel way. She had many children who all had children before day care was in vogue. As a rule, every grandchild was dropped off at her place during the day all summer long. As the matriarch, she was expected to take care of her eight grandchildren, and sometimes neighborhood strays, for free — alongside working the night shift at the chicken processing plant. DeShawn knew there is virtually no way to sleep during the day with eight brats in your house, and she got fired after her second year. Then she started charging her children for childcare.

• • •

DeShawn took long walks with his grandmother through the cotton fields and when her garden would bloom. As a child, he had never noticed how fucking hilarious she was. She had a laid-back, super-intellectual, dry humor that didn't register unless you really listened. She told him about her first time on an airplane just last year. "Shit, boy, that thing got to going and rocking in the air, and I sure thought Jesus was gonna take me then. I looked around, and everyone else was being cool so I said, 'Shit if everyone else gon' die cool, guess I'll die cool too!'" He marveled at it. DeShawn understood now where his humor came from, as his mother wasn't funny — she only had three gears: annoyed, serious, or loving.

The one day that could keep the two women he loved most from wringing each other's neck was rather obvious: Mother's Day.

DeShawn's mother gave a special Mother's Day sermon at the church, and dedicated it to her mother — it touched DeShawn and he started to cry. He wanted to see the two women have a day of love and peace.

After church the family collected at DeShawn's grandmother's, preparing to go out to eat. DeShawn could already taste the catfish on his lips, and went looking in his grandmother's room for a candy bar to tide him over till dinner — he knew where his granny hid her secret stash. After finding a Snickers in her top dresser drawer, DeShawn saw a picture on his grandmother's desk. It was his mother and aunts' elementary class photo from the sixties. A row of little black faces (the schools had not yet been integrated) and then his mother's face — so young he didn't really recognize her — and sitting to her right was Jatius's mom, Edna McClansy.

It dawned on DeShawn that he hadn't seen Edna *once* since he'd been home. The thought of her shook him like a very cold breeze. Three seconds later he heard his mother honk the car horn, signifying that they were leaving for the restaurant. DeShawn put the Snickers back in its place and hurried out to the car.

CHAPTER TWELVE

DeShawn decided the time had come.

He propelled his car up the highway and past the mountain range on his way to visit Edna McClansy. She stayed in town a year after Jatius's death, then moved an hour up the road to Chattanooga. No one had heard much from her since except for DeShawn's mother. They had been besties from elementary school up until the present, and still talked on the phone constantly.

"OH BOY, DESHAWN!!!" Edna greeted him over the phone with the love of a second mother. "You get your butt up here to see old Edna, you hear? I'll fry us some catfish!"

DeShawn knew he was a man that liked things feeling "equal," things coming full circle. He wanted this visit with Edna (a woman he hadn't seen in twenty-plus years) to feel, maybe not like closure, per se, but like symmetry—like a snake eating its own tail perhaps. Jatius had never left DeShawn's head; he could only imagine how Edna must feel. He stopped for gas somewhere up the state line thirty minutes shy of his destination when he got stuck on a conversation he had with his mother some time before.

DeShawn had admitted to his mother that Jatius McClansy molested him. He told her every detail, and after his confession stood silent, feeling naked. Her response was nothing short of exactly what his mother would say. DeShawn had always marveled at his mom's fury and also, in stark contrast, her coolness. These were the times her psychic-prophet side would emerge—wisdom falling out her mouth like a goddamn waterfall.

"Round about the time you were born, Jatius and a couple of other boys in the field were fondled by this man Randy that lived down by the river. We found out what he was doing to them and we ran him out of town real quick. Jatius thought what he did to you was right 'cause it happened to him. Forgive Jatius and forgive yourself—you can move on from this."

DeShawn's mother always spoke recklessly when it was unnecessary, and coolly when it was greatly needed. Forgiving felt like a radical notion to DeShawn, seeing as he couldn't say if he had ever *really* been mad at the other boy, but there was some tension there about what Jatius had done.

All DeShawn knew was that whatever he felt he was letting go of would become manifest as he knocked on Edna's front door and was greeted by a woman who looked so much older than he remembered. "DESHAWN BABY!!!!! COME GIVE MISS EDNA A HUG!!!" she said as he stepped in and obliged.

Edna's house was filled with Glade PlugIns smells, candles, black Jesus paintings and figurines, and plastic-wrapped furniture. It was spotless, dustless, and immaculate. He could smell fish frying and his mouth started watering.

"So I guess you gon' spend the night. I had John clean up the upstairs room for you. He said he'd take you out for drinks tonight so y'all can catch up. He's still at work," she said from the kitchen as DeShawn sat in the living room sipping the peach sweet tea she poured him. DeShawn tripped out at the fact that John, well into his thirties, was still living at home, but then again, so was DeShawn. *Oh, the damaged men of the field*, he thought.

DeShawn loved Edna McClansy and knew her well. She was from a house of five girls, and both her parents were run-of-the-mill field people. Not much trauma there, but when she was seventeen her father tried to marry her off to a boy whose family was a bit better-off than the rest of them. But after he got Edna pregnant he didn't marry her, and she had to raise baby Jatius alone. She still worked and got herself through college with nil resources, and later had John by some man no one really knew. She kept her job on the army base until the year after Jatius's death, when she moved to Chattanooga and became a nurse. She had done well for herself and looked good. She was a beautiful, dark-skinned woman, her hair natural and completely white. Yes, she had aged damn well despite the trouble written on her face.

DeShawn and Miss Edna kiki'd all night, about how John used to beat DeShawn's ass all the time, and that time he spent the night and she woke all of them up at 3:00 a.m. to clean the house. "Aw, honey, I was a stressed-ass black woman raising two boys by myself. Nigga, put yo'self in my shoes," she said, tickling herself to death.

"Do you ever miss Jatius still?" DeShawn asked. With a couple of beers in his system, he was too curious to stop himself.

"No, baby, it's not the same." She looked off. "You know, I didn't think he would ever do that and it nearly killed me when he did, but when I found out about what led up to it, I just got mad. I had fought so *hard*. I thought he understood that you can't give things away for free, not as hard as we got to fight." She looked at DeShawn. "But, no, I don't miss him the same way I did. I'll see him one day." And she left it at that. It was all DeShawn needed to hear.

DeShawn didn't blurt out his secret about Jatius. It didn't feel fair to mention it, and he knew that, besides his mother knowing, he could take that secret to the grave. He also was sure that on some level Jatius's absence spelled some form of meaning in his life. He couldn't shake the memory of him. He felt sad.

Twenty minutes later, who should walk in the door but DeShawn's old archrival John. He gave a quick hug and a hi, and then went to his room to change and escort DeShawn out the door in a hurry.

In the years that had passed, it turned out John had kept tabs on DeShawn. John was gay too and had seen DeShawn's dirty movies online. They made a beeline for Alan Gold's, the legendary gay club in Chattanooga. They did blow, watched a drag show, and gave each other blow jobs in the restroom.

Later they made it back to the house and fucked all night.

In the morning DeShawn woke with a massive hangover and snuck back to his room to mess up the bed so it appeared as if he had slept in it. He lay in the faux-disheveled bed and stared at the ceiling fan swirling over it. This new revelation was too damn intriguing for him. He decided to stay up in Chattanooga a couple more days. He knew Edna and John (particularly) wouldn't mind at all.

CHAPTER THIRTEEN

DeShawn woke up in Chattanooga three days after he was supposed to have left. It was a queer feeling. He wrapped his mind around the visceral facts: that morning a childhood enemy, who was also the younger brother of his first "lover," fucked his brains out.

What a mess, he thought as he collected his mind and went downstairs to make some tea.

Edna had left for the weekend on one of her bimonthly gambling pilgrimages to Biloxi. Before she left, DeShawn asked her if he could take a look at some of Jatius's things. She informed him there was a box of his old belongings in the downstairs closet. He braced himself for the moment when he would confront the contents of the box.

John had already left for work that morning, and DeShawn promised Edna he would bust up the dirt in her backyard to prepare for the sunflower garden she planted every summer. She grew magnificent sunflowers. They sometimes grew up to seven feet, yellow and strong.

He began steeping a packet of Earl Grey in a very hot cup and his mind was reeling. After Jatius's suicide, and after the McClansys had settled in Chattanooga, DeShawn was finally learning about John and what his life had been like.

John became a teenage raver of sorts. There were pictures of him in high school all over the house with dyed neon hair, wielding glow sticks and candy necklaces. His room still held artifacts from his teen years, old VHS anime cartoons and a forgotten stack of drum-and-bass records. He was even briefly a drag queen in his early twenties. There were pictures of him performing at the Toolbox (a gay club in Chattanooga) dressed like Beyoncé. The trajectory of his old childhood enemy after his older brother's suicide fascinated DeShawn to no end. He would not have seen the plot twist of John being gay too.

John had explained to DeShawn the reason he never left his mother's home. He was afraid of leaving her as she had, naturally, fallen to pieces after Jatius's death. It wasn't a very odd reasoning at all. He thought about John and Edna spending those years in arrested development, trying to move on from the tragedy. DeShawn cried a little into his teacup and then mobilized.

He grabbed a hoe from the back porch and began busting up the garden, pulling away the dried, dead weeds from the flower bed's last period of bloom. The garden wasn't a disaster — it just needed some tending.

He remembered the heart-to-heart he'd had with Edna before she left on the charter bus for Biloxi with the other older women. "You know, baby, people think life is all about the big battles, but it's really not about that. Sometimes it's about finding enough self-love just to get the day's chores done. If you can do that much every day, life gets a little easier every day."

He took this advice to heart and began the chore of gardening.

DeShawn loved light gardening, putting chaos into order. It was (of course) chock-full of metaphors for him — the clearing away of the dead, the planting of new things, the fact that the harvest was always somehow greater than what was planted. While hoeing and weeding, he thought about his inner landscape: Was his own garden watered and weeded enough? He was pretty sure it wasn't.

Earlier, he looked through John's book collection, and stopped when he found a book of

Greek myths. He and John shared a childhood love of those myths.

Before he left back home to Alabama for his uncle's funeral, DeShawn had a reading from a fortune-teller who used the Mythic Tarot, a deck based on the ancient Greek myths. The fortune-teller pulled his cards and explained that his life was moving from a Dionysian era into an Apollonian era. He was leaving behind the wild, dark, wine-filled nights and moving into a personal epoch of sunlight and general enlightenment. This sounded good to DeShawn, though he wasn't quite sure he felt Apollonian yet. In terms of archetypal Greek heroes DeShawn felt like a mix of Atlas and Sisyphus. Continually carrying the world on his shoulders to a great height and watching it all crumble and roll back down, just to put it back together and carry it again. He saw gluing his world back together as rest periods. The true power was never in reaching the summit, but when he was at the bottom repairing it. He thought of himself as his own divine sculptor. Could he ever really lay his burden down?

He kept on in the garden. The sunlight felt warm and nurturing on his body as he planted the sunflowers. *There has to be magic in this*, DeShawn thought. At least he hoped so.

DeShawn hurried along with his work. He

knew John would be home soon. The thought of sex between the two men tugged at him. He wondered if he was having sex with John just to be closer to the memory of Jatius. It was worth asking even if the scale of the two siblings was so different.

There was, of course, the Jatius of DeShawn's memory. He was a towering figure in both physicality and presence. Did he remember Jatius this way because he had been a young boy? It was hard to say. John, on the other hand, was just different. He was average height, boyishly featured, and had a roundness to him. He was in his early thirties, but still looked to be in his early twenties. He was softer in his mannerisms and speaking than DeShawn recalled — a far cry from the little hooligan that used to shout "faggot" at DeShawn and hurtle dirt clods at his head.

The day before, DeShawn and John took a trip up to Lake Winnepesaukah and then Lookout Mountain. They dropped acid and climbed through the mountains to look at the black-light-illuminated gnomes some crazy person carved into the rocks god knows when. DeShawn, again, was having a problem with memory and scale. He remembered coming to Lookout Mountain as a child and everything being bigger. Memory worked against time, which seemed to shrink everything, his biggest touchstones looking smaller and smaller in the distance.

John walked into the back garden and surprised DeShawn, who was moving weeds into a pile. "Good work, sexy boy," John said calmly. "Let's go eat."

They went to the Pickle Barrel downtown, whose specialty was fried pickles served with honey mustard. They chowed down, drank beer, and walked across the pedestrian bridge into North Chattanooga. John took DeShawn to the local fruit loop tucked in the woods where he went to hook up with older men when he was a teenager. They moved past some bushes and fucked in the woods, mosquitos making it a little difficult.

DeShawn wondered about John and Jatius. Specifically, he wondered if Jatius had done to his brother what he had done to him. It made him a little sick to his stomach to think about and almost dimmed Jatius's light in his head. The night before DeShawn left, he decided he had to say something. As he lay in bed with John, he asked him very directly. "John, Jatius never did nothing bad to you, right?"

"Bad?" said John, queerly furrowing his brow. "Naw, he beat my ass good a couple times, but naw man, my brother was chill . . ." and left the question right there. DeShawn decided he didn't want to press it.

That same night DeShawn descended the stairs to the hallway closet to explore the box of Jatius— things Edna pulled for him. There was a paper with his handprint he made in kindergarten, a Tupac shirt, a class ring, and a picture from ninth grade homecoming. He smelled the shirt and it didn't smell like he remembered Jatius. It had been washed clean of his scent years ago, and just smelled like an oak-lined closet. DeShawn shocked himself when he began to cry. He knew staying here this long was a mistake. He walked back upstairs to cuddle with John one last time and write a note to Edna thanking her for her hospitality before hopping in his car. By late morning he was back over the state line, home in Alabama.

CHAPTER FOURTEEN

DeShawn sat in his mother's living room, stoned off of shitty bammer weed, staring at his mother's collection of grade school pictures of him and his brother. They were very disturbing.

From the ages of five to twelve, whenever there was picture day at school, DeShawn's mother had the maniacal habit of waiting at the front door of their home, in her nightgown and rollers, brandishing a huge plastic jar of Vaseline.

"I don't want you lil' babies to be ashy in your pictures," she would say, annoyed and half-awake, as she smeared an ungodly amount of petroleum-based goop on their faces as they ran out of the house to the bus.

DeShawn sat in his mom's love seat looking at this bizarre collection of Olan Mills photographs, the faces of his brother and him greasy to the gods and sweating from the lights, goop clogging their young pores.

I've had a hard life, thought DeShawn as he went to the kitchen for a snack; he had a hellified case of the munchies.

There was this picture of him in eighth grade that he couldn't quite shake; he remembered the day too vividly. It was some time after Jatius McClansy had killed himself. It was a picture from middle school. In it, he was wearing a Foo Fighters T-shirt. Later that day, after they had taken the picture, he got sent to the principal's office for mouthing off.

Years later, as an adult, DeShawn learned what he had always felt was true but couldn't articulate—that a lot of schools in the Deep South still practice forms of segregation. In a middle school with close to a 40 percent black population, DeShawn was one of three black kids placed in advanced-placement classes. He was, as his father would lovingly put it, "a nigga who knew how to talk to white people." He was almost never placed with the two other black boys, and had to endure—for each subject no less—a class of thirty redneck motherfuckers saying the craziest shit one could imagine. Self-esteem was a hard battle to fight in these conditions, not to mention the white teacher who had tried to instill some sort of pride in him that day.

The incident was in Mr. Nash's social studies class. Mr. Nash was lovingly teaching revisionist history and skirting around the subject of slavery, though DeShawn couldn't tell if it was for his sake or Mr. Nash's. In the middle of his Southern-fried bullshit soliloquy, Mr. Nash looked directly at the class and said, with sympathetic eyes, "You know, this whole slavery thing has been really blown out of proportion. Think about it chullrin'—if you paid a thousand dollars for a man, would you treat him *bad*? That was a lot of money back then!" DeShawn let out a deep sigh and stopped listening. That was his fatal mistake.

Mr. Nash was red in the face and teary-eyed as he talked about the "war of Northern aggression," and side-eyed DeShawn doodling in his notebook. He slapped DeShawn's desk, startling the boy half to death, and proceeded to go in on the young artist.

"Boy, you are just doodlin' away! Just *doodlin'*! DOODLIN'! If you applied yourself you could be the next Martin Luther King Jr.!" he said, whole-heartedly proud of himself.

"But I don't want to get shot in the head," said DeShawn, rather sheepishly.

"GET TO THE OFFICE! YOU'RE GETTING A PADDLING!"

DeShawn was well into his twenties before he learned that corporal punishment was some bullshit that mostly went down in the Deep South; all his adult friends who grew up in California winced at the mere mention of it. DeShawn also marveled at how much of his young adult life was spent in a room getting spanked by a dirty old white man; by eighth grade he had been paddled some fourteen times. This was, he was certain, how he came to like this kind of scene. The main thing he took away from the Alabama Public School System was how to bend over and take the goddamn abuse. As an adult, this behavior had earned him coin one summer in San Francisco, but during his adolescent life it was mostly, quite literally, a pain in the ass.

The plot thickened.

The principal of the school was a goddamn queen from hell. He was an old-school faggot (meaning he had a wife and kids). At every pep rally he would put on a wig, impeccable makeup, white go-go boots, and a school sweater and pretend to be the new sex education teacher, Poopsie. DeShawn and his entire eighth grade class would go totally fucking bananas when he said "sex education."

The principal knew DeShawn's family all too well. He would say the same bullshit each time he paddled DeShawn. "Now DeShawn, you know that your great-granpappy used to raise chickens for my family. He stayed on our property for years," he would say in his high-pitched, musical Southern drawl. DeShawn vaguely remembered this property, as his great-granddad died when DeShawn was only about seven. All that was left of the old man's existence were photos and the old cinder block house in which he'd lived. Trees were growing through it now. DeShawn stared at the Principal's face. *Oh shit*, thought DeShawn. *He's about to start crying again.*

Sure enough, he did.

The principal started in with a face full of tears, "DeShawn, boy, I looooooooooved yo' granpappy, I swear fo' God, I looooooooooooved yo' granpappy. I stayed by his side every day for years. He would take me off fishing and hunting." He would go silent and stare off into the distance after this part, and then came the part that always made DeShawn's skin crawl. It was the way he always punctuated his speech: "You know, DeShawn" — long, sentimental pause — "You sure do look just like him." *Wink.*

DeShawn was too young to conceptualize the term "eye-raped," but surely it just happened.

In his later years, DeShawn began to wonder just *why* this spooky-ass cracker "looooooooooooved" his great-grandfather so much, and was certain he didn't want to know. He related this story to his older cousin, Tyrone, on the bus ride home.

"Aw, man," said Tyrone, shaking his head in disgust, "that crazy-ass faggot still say all that bullshit? He started crying too! Didn' he!" Tyrone was not having it. "Listen, he used to say that shit to Coby, LaMont, Jacob, Lulibelle, LaKeisha, Andre, Shantesa, Shavonne, NaTasha . . ." He began to list off their twenty-three other immediate cousins, and DeShawn stopped paying attention.

DeShawn would have another notable interaction with the principal near the end of the semester.

One afternoon, DeShawn jumped off a school bench to watch five girls brawl, and in doing so dropped the precious contents of his pocket: his 1995 Luis Royo X-Men Spring Break trading cards. The cards depicted renditions of Iceman, Bishop, Wolverine, Archangel, and the rest in tiny, slutty swimwear on the beach. All DeShawn knew was that looking at these comic book men in their underwear made his dick rock hard.

He heard through the grapevine that a teacher had picked them up and put them in the principal's office. He went to the principal and explained what he lost.

"Oh," said the principal, queerly, "you mean those cards with all the muscle men in their gymmie shorts? I saved them for you!" He went to retrieve the cards. "Now normally that type of thing ain't allowed in school, but I'll allow it this time," said the principal, winking. It was a different kind of wink—a loving one. DeShawn remembered it as an "I know you're queer as hell and it's okay" wink. In a way, DeShawn missed his creepy old principal.

DeShawn sat at his mother's kitchen table, stoned off his ass, eating Lucky Charms.

"All these goddamn memories," DeShawn said between spoonfuls of pure sugar.

CHAPTER FIFTEEN

DeShawn was sifting through his mom's junk drawer. He had decided to journal and was looking for a pen.

The drawer seemed holy to him.

While looking for a pen, DeShawn found a curling iron from the forties that had been in his family for generations (it was a high school graduation gift to his mother from his great-grandmother, and she had used it to straighten her hair before church since before god knows when), a pack of cards (his mother played competitive Spades with the other women in the neighborhood), old mail, bobby pins, old phone cords for a landline, and a baby picture of his younger brother. But the best find was a Polaroid of himself. It was taken in Texas nearly fifteen years before. He was wearing a Guns N' Roses T-shirt (for whatever reason, he hated Guns N' Roses), hooker shorts, and standing by a van in a gas station throwing up a peace sign. He had to have been eighteen, but looked younger. He was still youthful and unassuming. It was like he was seeing his own ghost.

Around the time DeShawn turned eighteen, he realized the state of Alabama wasn't big enough to hold what was inside of him. The last boy he touched was Skylar. His awkward preteen years bled into his awkward teen years, and now high school was over. Thank god. As near as he could tell, all DeShawn wanted to do was fuck boys and play in bands. That seemed as good a life as any, and he had set his eyes on the promised land: California.

An older punk gave him a copy of an underground music zine, *Maximum Rocknroll*. It was the 1992 "Queer" issue, and in it DeShawn saw a black drag queen in a cop outfit wearing a strap-on and faux fucking an underground genius punk porn director. "I have to get to California!" he screamed out loud on his porch, where he was secretly reading the contraband magazine, which his mom surely would have taken if she had found it.

DeShawn started subscribing to *Maximum Rocknroll*, as it had a personals section for kids looking to meet pen pals, and also one for kids who made zines.

It was a good five years before the computer age would kill the whole vibe of American youth making punk-rock Xerox connections, before people spilled their life in public posts, and before all this tawdry bullshit. DeShawn, like all the other maladjusted fuckheads he knew, spent hours on click-and-bang type-writers and even longer hours at Kinko's, stitching together all the random thoughts in his head. The zine was both a document and a calling card. It provoked the question, "What does your zine say about you?"

DeShawn met Kelly though zines. Kelly lived in Mobile, some six hours away. He made a zine about wanting to kill his parents and the president at the time, George W. Bush. It was pre-9/11 kicks at its finest. Kelly called DeShawn one day and said, "I'm blowing this joint. You wanna move to California with me?"

"*Yes*," DeShawn replied immediately. The farthest west DeShawn had ever been was Arkansas.

He hitched a ride down to Mobile with some punks he knew and got to Kelly's dad's house. Kelly informed him that the van they would be driving had a broken speedometer, no license plate, and no registration. In the van would be Kelly, his younger brother Jason, DeShawn, two dogs, guitars, records, bikes, and other things that would be impounded for life if a cop stopped them.

With two hundred dollars among the three of them, the men set sail.

Thirty miles outside of Mobile, Kelly fell asleep at the wheel and hit the side of the bridge, resulting in a flat tire. The three men got out to inspect the damage. They were slow to register that not one of them had ever changed a flat tire before.

Two burly rednecks stopped to help and, upon moving closer to the group of punk boys in distress, froze dead in their tracks. It probably never occurred to the boys that they dressed a bit like hookers. DeShawn was wearing a sleeveless crop top featuring a black Mickey Mouse, and jean cutoffs so short the pockets were hanging out, as well as his balls. Kelly, not one to be outdone, was also wearing a crop top with a lipstick emblem on it, purple denim hip-huggers, and a studded white belt with a buckle that read (in rhinestones no less) "Baby Girl." The rednecks stopped because, from the highway, the boys appeared to be slutty girls that needed help. In true testament to either Southern politeness or the power of just being too weird to fuck with, the redneck men shook off their repulsion and helped the young men with the tire. Within half an hour, the three were back on the road again.

By nightfall they reached Houston, and DeShawn realized that it was really happening. He saw the western expansion of the night sky, and Alabama was becoming this background static that was farther and farther behind him. He was leaving. And, in fact, had left.

The second tire blowout occured mid-Texas. The three spent Saturday night sleeping in a Walmart parking lot, waiting for it to open so they could buy a new tire and fix the spare. Morning came and it was revealed that this particular Walmart didn't open on Sundays because of some blue law. They decided to walk the dogs and wait in the parking lot until Monday.

Pastor Sam rolled up on the three men in a minivan and said that there was an open Walmart fifty miles away. He would drive two of them there if they gave him gas money and donated a small fee to the church he was trying to start in his native Mexican border town hours away. The three men agreed and within a few hours they were waving goodbye to Pastor Sam and speeding back down the highway.

It was a peaceful trip after that, save a run-in at a Whole Foods in New Mexico where they tried to scam sandwiches and were caught.

DeShawn was behind the wheel when they reached the sign at the Arizona border that read Welcome to California. He almost didn't believe it. He would forever remember the couple hundred wind turbines spinning near the southern border. The stark look of it stuck with him, as he had never seen wind turbines in a cluster before. It marked his mind. *Things must be different here*, he thought.

One more night of sleeping at a rest stop outside of LA, and then in the morning, they reached Oakland.

Kelly shook DeShawn something awful when they entered the Bay Area. "DeShawn! Look! It's the Dublin BART station! We're almost home!" DeShawn, not knowing what the fuck Kelly was talking about, rolled his eyes and went back to sleep.

CHAPTER SIXTEEN

DeShawn arrived in California mid-October, in a van full of weary travelers. His first home was a warehouse in the Fruitvale neighborhood of Oakland. The singer of a local dyke band led the house, and he felt at home. He often slept on the roof of the warehouse and was amazed at the sight of the fog rolling in from the Bay. It amazed him for the rest of his tenancy.

DeShawn was walking up San Leandro with Kelly's dog one day when a Goodwill truck honked at him and the driver pulled into an alley. The driver got out on the passenger side, his dick rock hard and exposed, and beckoned DeShawn to come over to him. DeShawn tied up the dog and gave the man a blow job in the truck. It had never occurred to him that a man would be so horny that he would behave this way, but it was just the beginning.

Two months later he moved to a new warehouse near the Alameda border. It was madness. It was a huge complex, sort of like punk rock dorms. Twenty kids lived there, and shared two kitchens, three living rooms, three bathrooms, a patio, and a huge carport where the house hosted punk shows for bands and stocked a vending machine that served beer for seventy-five cents. DeShawn crashed in one of the living rooms and sometimes slept on the unfinished wood floor, coughing sawdust through the Hello Kitty sheets he laid on the ground. All he could think about was how this place felt like heaven.

He made friends with all the random punks, drunks, and midnight philosophers, and even started a fling with a straight speed addict that lived down the stairs. Boys were proving to be a danger.

DeShawn would make a weekly pilgrimage to the Eagle Tavern in San Francisco, get wasted to all hell, and meet the wrong types of men. It was thrilling until the day Todd and Aaron showed up. They were these two white twinks who seemed fine at first, but proved evil. They all became friends too quick, and the next week the two came to DeShawn's warehouse to visit and smoke weed. Todd was the more forward of the two, and talked slick to DeShawn about his anatomy. "Damn, you're thick," he said as DeShawn was bent over, rearranging vinyl LPs in a stack on his bedroom floor. Aaron chimed in. "You wanna come with us to a cool spot in Orinda?"

"Sure," said DeShawn not really knowing where Orinda was but trusting the two for no good reason.

They set off in Aaron's car, with DeShawn in the back. The trip was taking longer than he expected, and before he knew it they were parked in some forest in god knows where, hiking through the woods.

"Let's stop here," Aaron said deviously. DeShawn was beginning to feel uncomfortable.

It was hard to see in the dark, but from what he could make out there seemed to be a cluster of trees with netting interlaced between them, and the figure of a man facing them, touching himself, and standing very, very still. DeShawn stopped dead in his tracks.

"What do you think you see?" asked Todd with this smile on his face.

It then occurred to DeShawn that he was in the woods of Orinda with two boys he barely knew and he was no longer in control. Why had he trusted them?

"I don't like this. I wanna go home," said DeShawn in probably the most serious tone he had ever used. Aaron and Todd put their arms around his shoulders on either side and walked him back to the car.

"It's okay, DeShawn, we were just trying to scare you," said Aaron, somehow lovingly. He never spoke to either of these boys ever again.

Some time later DeShawn met Mark, this cute black boy who lived up the street from the warehouse. He was walking to Popeyes when the boy called out from his porch, "Hey you! Come here!" DeShawn saw that the boy was handsome and obliged.

Mark lived with his white daddy. Not "daddy" in the biological sense but "daddy" as in the older gentleman he was fucking for money, love, and attention (though not in that order). Mark was keen on DeShawn's ass, "Damn, you're thick." DeShawn shrugged; he had heard it all before.

Mark introduced DeShawn to his daddy. The man explained, "Ever since my divorce from my wife I prefer the company of black men. My kids are grown, so I can do whatever the fuck I want." Though he seemed harmless, DeShawn still made it a point not to be left alone with this man.

Mark and DeShawn would fuck in the basement of Mark's daddy's house, between impromptu voguing battles and ogling 50 Cent on BET.

"Would you fuck that nigga?" asked Mark.

"Dude, I would *TOTALLY* fuck that nigga. I would let him get me pregnant — with twins," said DeShawn between puffs of the biggest fucking blunt, like, ever.

The two would sometimes discuss politics. "I hate the KKK," said Mark. "Oh my god, I *totally* hate the KKK too!" squeaked DeShawn.

Eventually, Mark got more into speed and the two boys didn't talk so much anymore.

Years later, DeShawn saw Mark in downtown Oakland, spun off his ass: shirtless, underwear and crack poking out of his cargo shorts, violently playing with his nipples at noon, and in broad daylight, humping a pole near Broadway and nineteenth. He was all turnt up.

Four years after that DeShawn saw Mark again downtown, pushing a stroller with three children very close in age.

"I just moved back from Kansas," Mark explained. "I'm a father now," he added.

DeShawn nearly shit himself with disbelief. He didn't judge Mark, he just thought about how funny and intense it was to witness the seasons of someone else's life. A week after the stroller incident, he saw Mark at the bathhouse, and they had sex. The whole time DeShawn wondered who the hell was keeping Mark's kids.

Some months after seeing Mark, DeShawn went to a "Gay Shame" protest. The political group was in the Castro protesting something or another (it was always *something* with them). That's where he met his future heartache.

DeShawn was fucked-up on MDMA, with a group of equally fucked-up queens, when an Indian man with a German accent, holding a camera, came up to him.

"I saw you dancing at the beginning of the protest. You are so lovely. I would like to paint you," he said. "My name is Michael." DeShawn was too young to understand this would be the beginning of the end. He obliged the man, and the years with him poured away like so much sand, the potential sifted into nothing at all.

One day the warehouse was to be evicted. There was a closing punk show to destroy the whole structure. DeShawn was wasted off his ass and came into the garage to watch a hard-core band play, and noticed the drummer was a cute little guy; the band sucked to all hell, but the drummer piqued his interest. Right as he moved to get a better look some random gutter punk crashed into him while mosh-ing, and instinctively DeShawn punched him in the face, hard. A fight broke out, the band stopped playing, and the two were pulled away. His nose was bleeding.

DeShawn went outside to pull himself together and felt a tap on the back; it was the drummer.

"Yeah, I hate gutter punks," he said as he handed DeShawn a red kerchief from his back pocket.

DeShawn, drunk off his ass, grabbed the boy by the face and started making out with him. The boy kissed him back.

"Let's go to my room," said DeShawn.

"Okay," said the drummer boy, giggling. "Don't you even wanna ask me my name?"

DeShawn rolled his eyes. "Okay, since it's so important to you — what's your fucking name?"

"I'm Arnold," he stated calmly, then giggled. "You're DeShawn. Everyone knows who you are."

CHAPTER SEVENTEEN

Back in Alabama, in the months after Uncle's funeral, DeShawn had almost played out whatever he needed to play out. It had happened that DeShawn was fooling around with Andre in his mom's living room one weekday morning while Andre's mom was at work. DeShawn was giving him a blow job and Andre took a video of the illicit act and saved it to his phone. The video went into an online cloud his mother could access, and Andre's mom called DeShawn's mom to let her know he was fucking her underage son. Right about a day later, as it was about to hit full-blown scandal, a phone call stole the thunder from the coming storm.

DeShawn's aunt called him from Harlem to let him know his biological father was dead. He would have to come to New York to clean out his dad's apartment, and help prepare things before his father's body went back to Alabama to be buried.

Oh lord, here we go, thought DeShawn as the plane peeled off the runway in Nashville en route to LaGuardia.

He went from the plane straight to Brooklyn. He would stay at his girlfriend's house to take the stress off his aunt in Harlem. Or rather, that was what was supposed to happen. DeShawn listened raptly as his girlfriend sat on a couch, got wasted, and bitched about the man she had been quasi-dating for eight years. She lamented that he hadn't asked to marry her, that he had a baby now, that he hadn't blah blah blahed. It took all his concentration not to fucking go off on her.

He met her in San Francisco, and they both had been punks in their youth. She confused him with all this ennui, and he wondered how the fuck she had enough faith left in men to expect anything from them. DeShawn looked at the pantheon of men in his life—all the fathers, uncles, fuck buddies, fake boyfriends, whatever—and they all felt like a void. They appeared out of nowhere and disappeared the same way, a puff of smoke. He was learning how not to want.

DeShawn had been drinking with his girlfriend for twelve hours straight. They both started bawling at an episode of an annoying black sitcom (some gay son on the show was having problems fitting into society so, naturally, they had to cry) and DeShawn got the notion to leave. His girlfriend, wasted off her ass, decided she didn't want him to go and started a long, abusive tirade. *"Why does every man feel like he gets to disappoint me?!"* It got so out of line DeShawn called the police on her, but soon realized he was drunk and yelling at a white woman in her own apartment. He knew what some New York cops were capable of; those egregious bastards would certainly barbecue his black ass for this one. He flew the coop, and it hit him that he just lost his father and now his best friend too. He had wanted to avoid staying at his father's place, but with nowhere to go he took the train to Harlem, to his father's abandoned apartment.

DeShawn's biological father and mother had met at a quaint, historically black college in Alabama—the same one Sun-Ra had been rumored to attend. They were never married; DeShawn had been a love child. And so his father had kept his distance. He was there for two weeks every summer, two weeks at Christmas, and some arbitrary spots here and there throughout the year. DeShawn remembered being about seven and his mother taking him down to southern Alabama to meet his father in some random hotel room by the highway.

His father was recovering from a gunshot wound and was living in DC at the time. "I was in DC buying crack, son," he explained to young DeShawn. "I was buying it from a boy not much older than you, guess he musta been bout twelve, I'll say. The bullet is still in me." DeShawn's father took his little boy's hand and rubbed it across his thigh; DeShawn could feel the bullet in his femur bone. His father felt like some sort of superhero.

DeShawn's father was not a peaceful man.

He always drank hard liquor when driving. Once when DeShawn came to visit him in Lamison as a boy, his father got drunk and wrecked the car they were riding in. The man and boy had to walk through the woods back to DeShawn's grandparents' house. "Are there werewolves, Daddy?" DeShawn asked. "There sure the fuck are, son. They're gonna get us any moment," said his dad. DeShawn held on to his dad's hand with an iron grip.

His father could be a complete asshole at times, which told DeShawn he came by this shared trait honestly. There were several times when his father drove them around the back roads of Alabama, nursing a cup of whiskey though strangely never swerving (he was quite a responsible drunk driver), and saying whatever the fuck came to his mind. "Me and your mother couldn't be together because your mother's a fucking whore," he often said. DeShawn was quite a bit older before he learned that a father should never talk to his little son this way, but DeShawn's papa was a man of few formalities.

One day after driving around, DeShawn's dad got even *more* drunk and took his son on a speedboat, and they sped and raised hell all over the Alabama River that afternoon. Later that night his father did what he always did when leaving his son alone in the pickup to get more liquor. "All right son, here's my gun." He handed teenage DeShawn a loaded hand-gun. "If any nigga comes starting shit you shoot 'um in his asshole, and when I get back I'll shoot 'um again." DeShawn hated the gun, and would always set it down and pretend it wasn't there.

DeShawn's father left Alabama some five years ago to move near his sister in Harlem. He also wanted to write.

Now, DeShawn had seen the signs that his dad was getting old before his years. He had been drinking heavily since his early teens, and when he turned middle-aged his health was already failing. The man had started to call DeShawn during blackouts; he would complain that his heart hurt, that people were poisoning him. He began calling his son and asking him to move closer, saying that they should get to know each other, that they had been estranged too long. DeShawn, then in his twenties, was having too much fun making mistakes in the Golden State to even consider it. "Dad's drunk again," he would say to himself when he received one of his calls. Then there were the times his father would call and be straight up belligerent and combative. All deep alcoholics are hard people to take care of and relate to. DeShawn wanted to forgive him, and he usually did.

He opened the door to his father's apartment. It was a small studio near 116th and Morningside. The smell hit him first. It was his father's smell—pork mixed with cheap cologne mixed with alcohol. It was a punch to the senses, and DeShawn wept. *Dad's still her*e, he thought.

The apartment was a mess. DeShawn's aunt told him about the minor heart surgery his father kept secret from him, but from the looks of the apartment it hadn't caused him to alter his lifestyle. There were loose Viagra pills all over the floor, alcohol in the kitchen, and three five-gallon jars of pickled pigs feet—his papa's favorite snack. These were all things contraband for a man with a weak heart. DeShawn's aunt explained. "Your father was ignoring his doctor's orders. We learned he had several stops at the emergency room a couple months before he died. He was depressed."

DeShawn put his father on a stretcher in his mind. He wanted to examine him. Here was a man who grew up with twelve siblings and watched his parents live to be ninety. He knew in his heart of hearts he did not want to be an old man. DeShawn was his raging spawn, psychically linked. He partied just like Daddy. The man must have seen his health failing, and all he had was himself and a quasi-estranged son in California. Who would have taken care of him if he lived to get old? DeShawn began to understand what the late-night phone calls demanding he move back were really about.

In the bathroom was another indication of his father's fear of mortality. The tub was stained dark with black hair dye, caked so hard it took days and a gallon of bleach to correct. DeShawn grayed early in his youth, and remembered his father freaking out about it, demanding he dye his hair immediately. Now DeShawn understood that it wasn't about his gray hair, it was more about his father having a son who was old enough to have gray hair. *That vain fucking bastard*, DeShawn laughed to himself.

The only tidy thing in the man's apartment was on top of his dresser—all the newspaper clippings and press DeShawn received as an emerging artist, all lined up in a row. The last thing he remembered his father saying to him, two months before he died, was that he was sorry they had gotten into whatever fight during the previous phone call, and that he loved him. This much would have to be closure.

DeShawn's dad had been an atheist for as long as he could remember. His father made fun of him for going to church. "I can't believe that your mama lets you believe in that bull-shit! You and the rest of them niggas sitting around in church giving that preacher money, thinking a white man is floating around in space and gonna punish you. It's disgraceful!" Saying it as if he were spitting out something horrible.

But as time came on, his father was alone, and like all dying men, started going to church—to find a wife, DeShawn suspected, as that's where all the middle-aged, divorced black women tend to congregate. On the first floor of his father's apartment was a Baptist church. DeShawn had partied to the gods one Saturday night and then rolled out the door on Sunday morning with bleached blond hair and Daisy Dukes, with all the women in the church side-eyeing him as if he were a burn-ing bundle of sticks. He had been there two weeks at this point, and knew he wasn't gonna be able to stomach too many more inquisitive looks from these good God-fearing assholes.

He didn't dismiss the Holy Rollers, though. DeShawn had his theories about it all. He would look at any moving body of water, a breeze stirring dead leaves, or a person singing to themselves in public, and he would *get it*. It wasn't hard to be reminded of God, or whatever the fuck one calls it. The feeling was everywhere; the problem was the million other moments of the day lacking this scale of epiphany. DeShawn trudged through the world with that hole in his heart, something missing. It was many things, but his father was one of them. He had been a ghost for years, but him actually being dead now made his absence more three-dimensional.

DeShawn didn't know how to explain his father — a man he called Father, but a man who was never really prepared to be one. Like so many men, it seemed like he'd just said, *Well, I have a dick — guess I should be a dad*, and learned soon thereafter his mistake. DeShawn grew up disbelieving in men, and perhaps vis-à-vis grew up disbelieving in himself. Either way, he went on the plane back to Alabama. The body was to be put in the ground.

DeShawn was always amused by how fucking drunk his dad's side of the family could get. The first night they congregated, they all got bombed on pineapple margaritas and DeShawn had to stop his two aunts from coming to blows, *and* had to stop himself from beating up his cousin. No ill will—they always forgave each other in the sober mornings. On the way to the church, DeShawn's younger, cool, fag-loving aunt gave him forty-three Klonopin and some sound advice: "Don't overdose, bitch."

Before the caravan left, it hit the boy hard. *Dad is gone.* He fell to the floor and cried until his older, more practical aunt came to get him. "Now, baby," she said, very lovingly, "Auntie's knees is bad and I can't come down there and get you. You got to be a big boy and collect your-goddamn-self." DeShawn got stuck at the words "be a big boy." In her head he was still probably five years old.

One of DeShawn's messier aunts whispered to him during the service, "You know, there sure are some sad hoes at this funeral," and motioned with her head to all the women in the small town his dad dated as a younger man. They were all sitting on the nonfamily side of the church.

DeShawn's father's side of the family was Lutheran, so the service was not like it would be on his mother's Baptist side. No drama or emotion, just stark plain and how-do-you-do.

His father's suit matched the casket, and DeShawn was a pallbearer. He wanted a hand in carrying his father to peace. He watched them lower his Papa Bear into the ground.

DeShawn and his fag-loving aunt went and got drunk in her pickup truck after the service. He popped one of the pills she gave him. All DeShawn could think was, *My daddy is dead, long live my daddy.*

CHAPTER EIGHTEEN

Deshawn woke up in a dark hotel room; staring at the whirling mass of blackness, he contemplated the void. Andre's dried cum was all over DeShawn's stomach, chest, and the edge of his mouth. It had been a fun reunion, though weighted. He felt parched and walked to the bathroom sink to clear his throat. He could feel his bad breath.

He turned on the light in the bathroom and saw the sleeping youth lying on his stomach, naked on the bed, Andre's lungs heaving up and down in a rhythmic sleep pattern. He felt like Psyche gazing on Eros for the last time.

He had been in New York for too long and had lost the boy's attention. The day before he flew back home to Alabama, he got a call from Andre saying that he had "finally accepted the Lord's call to preach," and that he had been "playing around with the spirit too much." He had found a girl his own age to date. Andre couldn't stop rambling about how he finally had a chance at the normal life God wanted for him.

He met DeShawn at a nearby Motel 6 off I-65 "one last time," and per usual they fucked like animals.

DeShawn gained some relief in this meeting. Andre's mother wasn't going to call the cops on him. Their fooling around was actually not that much of a scandal in a small town that had known so much. It was just another thing that happened, and it was on to the next.

When DeShawn looked at Andre all he could think was, *This young man doesn't know himself very well.* He stopped short after he thought it. He knew he was projecting.

DeShawn looked in the mirror and all he saw was a man who had been absent from himself. It was a learned behavior. Years of encounters like these hadn't left him hollow, but there was a feeling that his sexual self was, more often than not, on autopilot. Experience is the only teacher, really, and one can rack up an enormous bill along the way. DeShawn's PhD in Whoreology cost him, and he would be paying for some time. He didn't lament though — he held tight to the one thing his experiences had afforded him: wisdom. He gained knowledge of both other people and himself. The kind he wouldn't have had access to had he been locked away in some boyfriend'shouse or the confinement of celibacy. To DeShawn, this wisdom was worth its weight in gold.

He wondered when his real life would begin, when it wouldn't seem like a mixtape of disappointments he was either enduring or surviving.

His life and the men he encountered, the quest for their presence, felt like a series of random treasure maps he followed for no reason other than for something to do.

He would get the map, sail across the ocean, make it to the deserted island, dock the boat and swim to shore, cut through a jungle, find where "X" marked the spot, dig up twelve feet of dirt, and finally find the treasure chest. Only to open it and find another set of instructions. He was often told never to look for love—"It'll come to you"—but he personally couldn't think of one great explorer who had ever found anything by not looking for it. DeShawn thought about how comfortable people were with dropping platitudes as undisputed truth.

Sometimes he felt he had looked too much. It was like searching for the Fountain of Youth, or the City of Gold, a useless pastime. All he found was the Book of Excuses, written by every lover.

"It's not the right time," or, "I would love

you more if you were less like yourself," or his particular favorite, "Don't expect shit out of me—ever." There were so many people offering nothing and treating that nothing like it was a prize to be fought over. DeShawn felt like a veteran of some weird war who fought bravely and gallantly for *nothing*.

DeShawn dressed, left the youth sleeping in the room, and walked next door to the Waffle House. He wanted a waffle, and to clear his head.

He knew that though he had always wanted something out of these men, he couldn't ever really figure what. Or maybe it wasn't the men, but a feeling. It was always this thing that felt unexplained and out of reach. He couldn't picture it, and it scared him. He learned from a meditator friend of his that if you can't picture it with your mind, you can't achieve it. DeShawn longed for nice surprises, because there were things his mind couldn't sketch.

He made a list.

Many men had died or simply vanished from his life—Jatius McClansy, Arnold, Skylar, his father, his stepfather, the list went on. He made a list of the pros and cons of all these men. He noticed that the last con for each of them was, *He never really loved me.*

He drew another list with their names. The title of this list was, "What Would I Have

Gained If They Had Loved Me." DeShawn stared at the sheet, blank as a white wall, until the waitress came up and asked if he was okay.

The only thing he could think to write was, *A sense of victory*. It seemed like a pathetic reason. It *was* a pathetic reason.

They were all such a troubled goddamn bunch. Their love would have quite possibly destroyed DeShawn, and to be honest the inverse could just as well have been true. *Maybe I didn't lose anything*, he thought. *Maybe I broke even*.

He felt a way he hadn't felt in a long, long time. He felt new.

He knew it was time to go back to California.

CHAPTER NINETEEN

DeShawn had been back in California for about two months. It was a very warm February — all around Oakland people were wearing shorts and carrying on like it was summertime.

DeShawn sat on a bench near the tidal lagoon of Lake Merritt and saw the joggers and baby carriages pass by, and sea gulls dropping the clams from midair to break the shells and feast. He had missed California with all his heart and was glad to be back home.

He had talked to his mother earlier that day. Church service had been canceled and most of the Tennessee Valley was covered by a blizzard — three feet of snow and climbing. He could picture the serenity of it all — beautiful and deadly looking.

He remembered kissing his mom goodbye as he walked to the plane terminal, where he blurted out of nowhere, "Mom, do you think I'm a whore?" She shook her head silently, kissed him, and gave him the redeeming caress of a mother's hug. "I want you to go back to California and know your own peace," she said. They'd talked every day since.

It had been about a year since his father's death and two years since Arnold's and DeShawn's uncle's. He could still feel the trauma in his body—the way it took extra coaxing to leave the bed in the morning—but these things were becoming fainter noises in the background. Would their slight static ever turn into silence? There was a hope.

DeShawn had called Michael the day before to catch up. He had divorced the younger art student. The whole thing had not even lasted a year, but Michael was on to the next, some other man DeShawn's age. Michael ended the phone call asking if DeShawn wanted to make love later in the week. He declined and decided never to call Michael ever again, but also not to look back in anger. He simply never looked back. It was devastating.

The day's errands flowed steadily. He looked at his watch and saw he had enough time to make it to the grocery store, acupuncture, and then his shrink.

He caught the eyes of all the bachelors wandering around buying organic whatnots, and looked in his own basket and saw that he, too, was part of the problem; there seemed to be nothing to do but shop. He went to the grocery store every day, like his version of what he was told European village life was like. DeShawn had been fucked by Sven again three days before and again looked at the man's floor covered in discarded fast food bags and burrito wrappers. DeShawn finally stopped judging Sven long enough to appreciate him for being a consistent fuck buddy — a measure of good character in its own right. He thought about it while they held each other after sex. It was the first time that DeShawn had had sex in a long time where it didn't feel like something was missing, like he was learning a gradual acceptance, though of what he wasn't quite sure.

He left the grocery with sixty-three-dollars worth of desserts. He had been eating a lot of desserts. It felt good.

DeShawn trotted down the sidewalk and into the sliding-scale acupuncture clinic. When he looked at his body all prodded with needles all he could think of was whichever saint it was that had all the daggers piercing them, and how he had to hold the position. He quickly moved to other metaphors; he didn't want to think about religion for a long, long time.

DeShawn made his way to the shrink. He sat in the lobby looking at all the other people in the waiting room and wondering what the fuck was bugging them. He seemed, for a second, invested in thinking about the world of problems outside himself. He came back to himself as his name was called into the office.

With that little bit he breathed in, let go, and propelled his soul and flesh forward; none of the worry seemed that important anymore.

When he left, he called his mother from a pay phone, just to feel nostalgic.

"Mama, I think I just had a major break-through," he said.

THE END

The Feminist Press is a nonprofit educational organization founded to amplify feminist voices. FP publishes classic and new writing from around the world, creates cutting-edge programs, and elevates silenced and marginalized voices in order to support personal transformation and social justice for all people.

See our complete list of books at
feministpress.org